The Triskele Galaxies

The Triskele Galaxies

Book Two
The Gossamer Sphere

by Melissa Conway

Chapter One

County Wicklow, Ireland

Under grey winter groundcover, shoots of spring growth lent a tinge of green to the Irish countryside. The cloudless sky would have been blue today if it weren't for the lingering haze of volcanic ash polluting the atmosphere since the Cataclysm. The spring season worldwide had been delayed from the resulting temperature drop. The Cataclysm had effectively halted global warming, but the cost was incalculable.

Kevin Guzman waited in his parked rental car, partially shielded from the road by a copse of evergreen bushes. Once the old man in his rusty red truck went by, Kevin pulled back onto the narrow country road and turned down a dirt driveway. He drove through a cloud of dust and exhaust from the old man's passing to a wooden gate marked "Private," which stood open and unattended. Under a thin canopy of bare, interlaced branches, the car bounced over ruts and through potholes. He stopped in the circular gravel driveway of a sprawling, one-story farmhouse.

With the old man gone, Kevin figured there was no one to answer his knock, but as a courtesy, he rapped on the iron-strapped oak door anyway. Then, following his compass and a mental map, he walked a thin footpath around the house to the northeast section of the property.

This was the sixth location he'd scouted in as many days, after three weeks of studying the geology of the region and poring over historical maps of the mines of the Emerald Isle. He saw what he was looking for behind a chest-high tangle of bracken that clung to an exposed cut of buckled sandstone and shale at the base of a low hill.

Scattered in the vicinity were overgrown piles of "tell," artificial mounds of cast-away rock. Partially buried nearby he found a smooth stone, the kind you'd see on the shore of a lake or beach; out of place here in the

1

hills. Examination of the stone revealed a worn groove, or "rill," where it had long ago been tied to a stick or bone for use as a hammer.

He unfolded his new portable axe and took a few whacks at the bramble, surprised to find most of it was loose. He looked closely at the severed stem of one; it was still a greenstick—someone had recently cut the bushes down and then replaced them against the rock wall. With an uneasy feeling, Kevin pulled the bushes away until the sandstone face was revealed.

Beginning in the Bronze Age and continuing up until explosives were invented, "firesetting" was an effective method of mining. Fires were set up against the rock face to heat it, and then doused with water to fracture the stone for extraction of the ore. The process left telltale depressions in the hillside.

In this day and age, an active mining society prowled Ireland's mines – big, small and insignificant. Even so, he'd heard about the existence of this place yesterday in a pub in the small village of Hollywood.

He'd been driving back to Dublin from a mine site when traffic had been stopped by the security guards for a film crew, of all things. In a broad field dotted with trees, a horde of painted men spurred their horses at a signal from the director. The scene must not have been pivotal to the plot, because all they did was ride a short distance, sweeping past one camera on a dolly at ground level and another up on a platform. Security waved the stopped cars on as the horsemen rode back to the start point for the next take.

The unscheduled delay prompted Kevin to stop for lunch at a pub in the mosquito-sized village. When the chatty waitress heard he was interested in historical mines, she told him about a crotchety old farmer who came in nearly every afternoon and stayed until he was blotto. The old guy had been complaining about the historical mine society salivating over an ancient opencast mine on his land.

"He won't let anyone go see it, though," the waitress said. "He's not very sociable, if you know what I mean. Makes a person wonder exactly what it is he grows on that farm of his, besides potatoes."

Now at that very farm, Kevin didn't see any suspicious-looking plants that would explain the farmer's unfriendliness, but he took a quick look around to make sure no one was watching. Other than bare trees swaying in the mild breeze and a flitting brown bird or two, nothing moved. The tunnel was low even for his stocky, 5-foot 4-and-three-quarters frame, and deeper than it should be. It might have begun as an opencast mine, but successive generations must have used better techniques to get deeper to the ore. Bending down to enter, he ran an eye over the walls and floor for evidence of recent habitation. He was no tracker, but if it weren't for the pre-cut bushes at the entrance, he'd think the cave hadn't been visited by humans since the erstwhile miners had abandoned it.

His eyes adjusted quickly as he went farther in. A normal person would have needed a light, but Kevin had recently come to terms with how very normal he wasn't.

Almost from the moment he entered, he knew this mine on the south side of nowhere was what he'd been searching for. At the end of the tunnel was a small cave, not much roomier than the tunnel itself, but at least he was able to stand upright. He couldn't imagine living in this claustrophobic space for six years, but that's what the lore said his grandfather had done.

Tadg the Small had been banished from the clan for his part in the deaths of six miners who were exposed to the very substance Kevin now sought. In this place, this *historic* place, not that anyone would ever know about it, Tadg had become the very first shapeshifter.

Kevin shivered a little as he imagined his grandfather's ghost haunting this seemingly insignificant cave. Unlike others of his kind, Tadg had lived only a few hundred years before his enemies took an axe to his skull and dumped his body in a bog. Kevin had seen what was left of his mummified, distorted torso on display in Dublin just weeks ago. While he'd bowed his head in respectful silence, mourning a man he'd never known, a British tourist loudly explained to his wife and two kids that Clonycavan Man had been sacrificed to appease pagan Celtic gods.

Not one to speak up under most circumstances, Kevin had to clamp his lips shut against a hot denial. Tadg had been a respected druid, and despite what the Romans two thousand years ago would like everyone to believe, druids did not sacrifice anyone. It had been a clan enemy who'd struck the fatal blows and disposed of the evidence in a most convenient and popular place—one of the peat bogs peppering the British Isles.

Kevin didn't have to examine the rock walls; he sensed the exact spot where his grandfather had found the iridium biometal that was used to craft the gossamer crown. He ran his fingers over the rock, feeling the chisel marks in the stone. Even if the bushes out front hadn't given him a clue, he could see someone had been here, and recently. They'd taken samples from several spots inside the cave, and that was a very, very bad thing—exactly what he'd come here to prevent.

He took in a deep breath of the stale air, closed his eyes and spread his hand over the rock.

"To me," he murmured, the same phrase he'd instinctively uttered the first time, when he'd drawn the microscopic biometal out of a deep-sea

3

core sample, leaving behind nothing but sand. That was nine months ago, at the start of the Cataclysm.

Kevin didn't understand the biological mechanism that allowed him to pull the iridium out of solid stone. Caitlin would probably know, or at least, as both a shapeshifter and a scientist, she'd have a better idea how he accomplished it. He suspected he was able to employ some kind of magnetic field through his palm, since Caitlin said iridium was attracted to magnetic fields.

When he'd removed every last trace, he tucked the resulting sunflower-seed-sized kernel of metal into his pocket and, with a last look around at his grandfather's former living quarters, bent down and headed for daylight.

The tunnel entrance was darker than it should be, so he craned his neck to look up. A chill of apprehension ran through him—someone stood there. Lit from behind, the shadowy figure looked menacing.

Kevin reached out with his gossamers, but before he could connect with the intruder's mind, a female voice with a mild Irish lilt said, "You're not one of the others."

He dropped into a squat. It was too late to shapeshift now that she'd seen him, but he decided on a dog in case it came to that.

As to what she said, Kevin presumed she was referring to whoever carved those chunks out of the cave. "How do you know?"

He could see her face now. Huge hazel eyes dominated the rest of her delicate features. She wore some kind of patterned bandana over her hair, and one of her cheeks dimpled when she smiled. "Because *they* were stylin' Hazmat suits. So what're *you* doin' on my land?"

"Your land?"

"Ah," she said with a backward tilt of the head. "You've met me grandfather. He spins a fine tale when he's had a few, doesn't he now? Are you here to catch sight of a leprechaun then? Or maybe one of the wee fairies known to flit about these parts?"

"I'm, uh-"

"American. Yes, I can tell from your accent. We're not savages. We do get cable out here."

"I didn't-"

"Well, you didn't have to say a word, did you?" She swept an arm to indicate the wild beauty of the land. "We may not live like kings as you do in America, but we've got an amenity or three."

Kevin clamped his mouth shut. She tilted her head, and he thought at first that she was waiting for him to speak so she could interrupt again, but

4

then he heard it—the distinctive whup-whup-whup of helicopter blades. The pointed ends of her bandana blew forward in a sudden breeze.

"They're back," she said.

Kevin didn't ask who. There was more than one organization interested in the biometal, but last he heard, Bill had been working with the British Health Protection Agency. They may not have the resources to fly to remote sites by helicopter, but other branches of that government certainly did.

Over the girl's shoulder, he saw it drop into view, engine whining loudly not a hundred yards from where they stood. In the copilot's seat, dressed in a Hazmat suit without the head gear, he spied a familiar face: Bill Masters, former head of the scientific drill ship that recovered the first sample of the biometal from the North Sea.

After Kevin's last encounter with Bill, he suspected things were about to get unpleasant fast. Speaking loudly enough to be heard over the noise, he told the girl, "If they find me here, it won't be pretty. Do me a favor. Hide my clothes."

She gave him a strange look before shielding her eyes with a hand and turning to watch the helicopter. Kevin didn't wait for her to agree; he put the biometal kernel under his tongue and within seconds, shifted. He shook himself out of his clothes and trotted to the girl's side. She looked down at him and then her head swung around to the pile of clothes. She met his doggy eyes with her own, and Kevin spared a brief moment to wonder how her eyes could possibly get any wider. But she bent and quickly rolled his shoes, socks and shirt into his jeans, lifting the bundle and clutching it to her chest as the chopper blades slowed.

Kevin sat back on his haunches as Bill got out and approached, the loose fabric of the older man's orange Hazmat suit flapping in the wind. He was followed by a man dressed like a soldier in fatigues, holding a rifle at the ready. The man stopped several yards behind Bill, looking at the girl as if she were a threat. Kevin felt a growl build in his throat.

"What are you doing out here?" Bill asked. "Your family was told specifically to stay away from this area. It's for your own safety."

She laughed. "Me grandfather was given a cock-and-bull story about unexploded ordnance from some war or another. Could ya not come up with somethin' a bit more intelligent? I don't see how your thin little suit's gonna protect ya from a bomb blast, Mister...?"

"Masters. And it's not safe out here, despite what you think."

"I'm not afraid to die, Mr. Masters. For that matter, maybe I'm interested in fast-tracking it." She wedged the bundle of Kevin's clothes under one arm and reached up to pull the bandana from her head, exposing white skin stretched so thinly over her skull Kevin could see the meandering trails of blue veins.

Bill stepped closer, a menacing mask over his handsome features. "It wouldn't be a quick or a pleasant death."

"Neither is leukemia."

Kevin desperately wanted to read Bill's mind right then, but couldn't take the chance. If Bill noticed the girl's very large 'dog' staring at him, and then noticed something was not quite right about said dog's eyes, Kevin's cover would be blown. In fact, the longer the girl stood there arguing, the more likely it was Bill would get suspicious.

Kevin stood on all fours and leaned his body into the girl's leg. She looked down and he gave a little "whuff," and trotted a few yards in the direction of the house. For a moment, he thought she was going to ignore his prompt, but she said, "Fine, then, Mr. Masters. I'll leave you to your mysterious business."

She took one step and Kevin, with his enhanced canine hearing, caught the sound of a small, dusty thud, knowing right away it was his wallet, which must have slipped out of the pocket of his jeans and landed in the dirt. He spun around with the intention of getting to it before Bill—but Bill was already bending with extended arm.

Kevin's heart began hammering in his chest as Bill straightened up, flipped the wallet open and saw Kevin's driver's license. His surprised brown eyes went straight to Kevin the dog, who dug his claws into the ground and shot off into the bushes.

Chapter Two

Lizbeth Moreau had no idea who Steven Muller was, but he must have been important, because someone named a building after him. The building in question, with its weathered grey brick walls striped with rows of dark-tinted windows, seemed too unprepossessing to house a prestigious agency like the Space Telescope Science Institute.

Not that Lizbeth had ever heard of STScI before today. According to Caitlin, her grandmother, the scientists, engineers and administrators who worked at STScI coordinated the use of the Hubble telescope, among other things. She and Caitlin were supposed to be on a 'getting to know you' sort of vacation, but Caitlin had surprised her with a visit to the peaceful Johns Hopkins University campus in Maryland. She'd said it was only a detour; that she needed to chat with one of the STScI astronomers.

"She's an old friend," Caitlin told her in their hotel room. "We attended university together before Hubble was even launched. I want to talk to her about Arp 274, find out if there was anything unusual about their data."

The triple galaxy group known as Arp 274 was imaged by Hubble in 2009. More recently, a similar triple galaxy was seen by their friend Kevin – only he saw it not in one of the enhanced photographs released by NASA to the public, but in his own mind.

He'd mentioned once that the image he'd taken away from his mental encounter with the alien entity had burned itself into his mind. It took weeks before he could close his eyes and not see the triple galaxies, which he was certain was represented by the triskele symbol on the gossamer crown.

"Isn't your friend going to wonder why you're asking?" Lizbeth asked Caitlin.

"She'll certainly ask, and I will lie."

"Do you expect there to be something unusual?"

"After everything that's happened? Why wouldn't I?"

Now, standing under an overcast sky with Caitlin outside the Muller building, Lizbeth watched Dr. Indira Gupta approach.

Indira wore a burgundy sweatshirt with the letters STScI embroidered on the breast. A thick black braid with a thin streak of white off one temple hung forward over her right shoulder. Her voice had no trace of an accent as she stopped a yard or so away and said, "Caitlin. You haven't aged a bit."

Lizbeth caught the faint look of chagrin that passed over Caitlin's permanently youthful face. She didn't know how long it had been since her grandmother had seen Indira, but it must have been long enough that she should have appeared before her as an older woman. Then Caitlin grinned, creating laugh lines around her eyes that hadn't been there before.

"Neither have you," she replied.

With a wry twist of her lips, Indira grabbed her braid and flopped it around. "Except for a rather noticeable loss of methionine sulfoxide reductase."

"A *and* B?" Caitlin asked with a lift of her brows that produced new furrows in her forehead.

"You know it."

Caitlin flipped her own curly, shoulder-length hair back in a girlish gesture. "You should go red. Henna has no cancer-causing coal tars."

Lizbeth had only the slightest idea what they were talking about, but she knew Caitlin didn't need to dye her hair. The henna comment was probably intended as misdirection to convince Indira that her naturally red hair had also gone grey, and she was now forced to color it.

Indira made a "tch" sound and said, "Not me. Naphthoquinone sensitivity."

Just as Lizbeth came to the conclusion that the conversation had entered some kind of scientist-speak one-upmanship contest, the two older women burst out laughing and fell into each other's arms. After they exchanged an enthusiastic hug, Indira held Caitlin by the shoulders at arms-length and exclaimed, "You're still an emaciated little thing, too! How do you do it?"

"Stress," Caitlin said immediately.

"Well, if we could isolate your particular brand of stress and put it in pill form, we'd be rich."

8

Caitlin reached an arm out for Lizbeth and pulled her forward. "This is my grand-daughter, Lizbeth."

Indira didn't comment on the obvious difference in color between Caitlin's alabaster skin and Lizbeth's light brown. She simply shook Lizbeth's hand and said conspiratorially, "Your grandmother is the smartest woman I've ever met."

"*Woman?*" Caitlin asked.

"Oh, person – person, of course." With a wicked chuckle, Indira said, "Although, there was this one incident involving a pig in the dorm that didn't reflect positively on a certain undergraduate's intelligence."

Lizbeth turned wide on eyes on Caitlin. This was a side of her strict and serious grandmother she'd never dreamed existed.

"I deny any culpability," Caitlin declared. "Certain alleged swine may have been seen, by persons of dubious repute, running out of my dorm room, but no proof of my involvement was ever found."

"No *pig* was ever found. I saw the darned thing myself, squealing down the hall, and to this day I'd like to know how you did it."

Lizbeth hid a smile. Indira, like most of Caitlin's friends and acquaintances, did not know Caitlin was a shapeshifter, or she wouldn't have to ask how the pig had "disappeared."

Caitlin changed the direction of the conversation by asking, "Have you been busy?"

Indira sighed. "Oh, yeah. The HEMP knocked three of the TDRS satellites out of orbit. Luckily HST wasn't affected, although the magnetic reversal has done some interesting things to the Van Allen belt."

"A HEMP?" Caitlin sounded mildly astonished. "Is that what you think it was?"

"What else could it have been?"

"What's a HEMP?" Lizbeth asked. "And TDRS and HST and ABCDEFG?"

Indira laughed. "Sorry. HEMP is an acronym that stands for high altitude electromagnetic pulse, which is when a nuclear device is exploded in the upper atmosphere to create a pulse to disable satellites."

"Which there was no evidence of," Caitlin interjected.

"Yet I have it on good authority the Air Force thinks that's what it was. Anyway," Indira turned to Lizbeth, "to finish answering your questions: TDRS is the relay satellite system used to communicate with HST, which stands for Hubble Space Telescope. I'm surprised your grandmother hasn't taught you all about this stuff. I seem to recall she used to be gung-ho about all things astronomy. Then poof! She just disappeared."

9

The corners of Caitlin's mouth lifted in a secret smile, but she didn't take Indira up on the hint to fill her in on what had been so important she'd been willing to completely abandon her studies. Lizbeth knew it probably had to do with Caitlin's decades-long search for the gossamer crown, which they'd literally unearthed just in time to stop the Cataclysm.

"So was Sam able to do those calculations for me?" Caitlin asked.

Indira stared at Caitlin for a fraction too long, and Lizbeth knew she was suspicious. To break the silence, Lizbeth asked, "What calculations?"

"The Arp 274 triple galaxy that Hubble imaged recently is about 120 megaparsecs away. Your grandmother asked us to determine what the galaxy triplet would look like today, which," Indira gave Caitlin a perplexed look, "she has to know we can't do. There's no way to accurately calculate such a thing – we can only speculate."

Lizbeth bit her lip and looked at Caitlin, trying to remember from science class what distance a parsec was.

"It's the same as 400 million light years," Caitlin explained. "Which also means the image Hubble got was what the triple galaxy looked like 400 million light years *ago*."

"Right, right," Lizbeth said, remembering. "Because it takes that long for the light from those galaxies to get to Earth."

Indira nodded. "We are essentially looking back in time, as we understand time, whenever Hubble observes an astrological body."

Then she directed that perplexed look Caitlin's way again. "I'm trying to figure out why, in times like these, you'd reappear like a ghost and request such a frivolous, yet resource-consuming favor. What are you *really* here for?"

Chapter Three

San Francisco, California

Zach Wong had almost finished his early morning five-mile run. He'd followed his usual route ten blocks down from his house, through the wooded area between his subdivision and the burnt-out housing project, around his old high school, and back again. He'd just gone past a patch of weed-infested grass in the little park a block away from his house where the sprinklers hadn't been adjusted since before the Cataclysm. One broken sprinkler head shot a stream of water ten feet into the air, and he glanced down to avoid the resulting puddle. The sun was rarely seen these days, and today was no exception. There were no shadows on the cracked sidewalk to alert him, but he sensed he was not alone.

Whoever it was approached swiftly and silently; other than the *shush* of the sprinklers, the only sound Zach heard was a harsh, "*Caw, caw!*" coming from the park. He didn't even have time to look around – just sent his right elbow up and back, connecting hard with the side of the man's head.

"*Ow!* Bloody Hell!"

Zach recognized the voice. He spun around, a smile already forming on his face.

"Seamus! What are you doing here?"

"Getting my head bashed in, it seems. Glad you missed my nose; it's been broken so many times, it's liable to fall right off my face if it takes another hit."

"Sorry about that. I'm a little jumpy since I started at the academy."

Seamus tugged on the band holding his dark hair back, removing it so the blunt-cut edges swung forward and brushed his jaw. He smoothed the spot mussed by Zach's elbow and re-bound his hair in its customary ponytail. "So you're almost a copper, eh?"

11

"Yeah." Even as Zach confirmed it, it didn't seem real. He'd had a vastly different set of plans for himself before the Cataclysm. In these times, a career as a video game designer seemed beyond frivolous.

"Well, rookie, you've got your work cut out for you. I haven't seen San Francisco this bad off in a hundred years."

Zach could easily imagine Seamus, with his deliberate, almost fastidious manners, dressed in turn-of-the-century garb, surveying the earthquake-devastated city while holding a lace-edged handkerchief to his face. "Oh, you like what we've done with the place? The decorator was going for postmodernism chaos."

Seamus laughed. "I forgot how amusing you can be."

He looked up at a large black bird cawing from the bare branches of a tree. "Is that your pet raven?"

Zach nodded and began to walk towards his house. "His name's Caw."

Seamus fell into step beside him. "We used to use ravens as spies back in the day. Did you know?"

"Yeah, Caitlin mentioned it. He's actually been a big help to me. Before I started training, I was deputized, like in the old west. It was pretty bad around here right after. Lot of violence, gang wars."

"Why did you stay? There are safer places."

Zach smiled and shook his head. "My family refused to leave. We've got deep roots in this area – mostly in Chinatown."

"Just because your family's here doesn't mean you can't travel. Have you never had the urge to see the world?"

Zach wondered what prompted the question. Seamus seemed more intent on his answer than mere curiosity warranted, but Zach said, "Nope. I don't ever plan to leave. I'm a homebody at heart. This is where I belong. I think I joined the force not just because I have the skills to do the job, but because I really want to help bring the area back to its former...glory, if that doesn't sound too dramatic."

"Nowadays, it's hard not to be dramatic."

They walked in silence for several yards before Seamus spoke again. "I need your help."

Zach's only show of surprise was a quick lift of his eyebrows. He hadn't been acquainted with Seamus long, but after everything the shapeshifter had done to help them stop the Gossamer Sphere, he trusted him implicitly. He couldn't imagine what the centuries-old bard wanted from him, however.

"Uh, sure...with what?"

"Well, I've got a little problem."

Zach glanced up and froze. Seamus had shifted as they'd walked and was now wearing a completely different face – a face Zach recognized from years of seeing it on the jacket covers of his favorite books.

Harcourt Quincy Spencer's fantastical tales had been a strong influence on young Zach. He'd read and re-read every book in the children's fantasy series *The Weredragons of Foggy Keep*. Each Halloween for five or six years, he'd dressed up as one of the characters. He still had the entire figurine collection, the prince and princess, evil Overlord O'Shay, and the knights of the moat that converted into weredragons with a few twists of their plastic limbs. He'd even sculpted the Keep out of cardboard and paper mâché, drawn the characters, cut them out, attached them to Popsicle sticks and written a play. Presenting it to his classroom to accolades from his schoolmates and an "A" from the teacher had been the highlight of the sixth grade.

"What are you doing?" Zach asked. "Why are you H.Q. Spencer?"

Then it occurred to him that Seamus, known on his former internet presence as Seamus the Bard, was a talented storyteller who could shift into anyone he chose. He might actually *be* H.Q. Spencer.

"H.Q. is going to be one hundred years old next week," Seamus said with a little sigh. "I need help killing him off."

"You're him? And you want me to – kill you?"

"Not for real, obviously. I need your help faking my death."

Zach frowned and began walking again. "Why don't you just have him disappear?"

"Most of my incarnations have in the past, but H.Q. has been profitable, and I've come to rely on his royalties."

"So you left the money to…yourself?"

"Brilliant, eh? Although technically I left it to my heir, whom I created not long after the cataclysm. A writer, of course, to carry on the tradition. Young, good-looking. There'll be a lot of sad female fans to console. But if H.Q. just disappears, his heir will be under suspicion, and the inheritance will be held up in probate waiting for seven years to pass, or some such nonsense."

They'd reached Zach's parents' house and stopped halfway up the front walk. Caw chose that moment to zoom in and land on Zach's shoulder. The bird fluffed his glossy black feathers and turned his head this way and that to get a good look at 'H.Q.' Caw had met Seamus before, and Zach suspected the canny bird knew exactly who H.Q. was, despite Seamus' appearance.

Seamus' hair, which was now thin and white and combed over to hide his freckled bald spot, blew forward in the morning breeze. Even knowing it wasn't really H.Q., or rather, knowing H.Q. was really Seamus, Zach had to fight against hero worship.

"I assume you have a plan?" he asked.

"Of sorts. You're rather integral to its success."

"Yeah, okay, I guess I can help, but right now I have to get a shower before going in to class. Believe me; I do *not* want to be late."

Seamus held out his hand and Zach shook it. H.Q.'s fingers felt crooked and frail.

"Thanks, Zach. I knew I could count on you."

"No problem. Just – before H.Q. kicks the bucket, can I get his autograph?"

Chapter Four

County Wicklow, Ireland

Kevin wasn't a big guy, but he was bigger than most dogs, and the size-constraints of shapeshifting limited his choice of breed. As a 160-pound Great Dane, he had long legs and was able to produce a fast run, but he also provided a big target. As he tore through the bushes toward the house, he heard Bill yell, "Stop that dog!"

Then, "*No!* Don't *shoot* him!" But it was apparently too late; a loud *crack* rang out and almost simultaneously Kevin felt a burning sting along his backside. He let out a frantic yelp, but kept running, waiting for the next shot to take him down. Ahead of him was a small building—a chicken coop. He left the dubious cover of the bushes to cross an open space between him and the coop. Chickens went flapping and clucking in all directions as he skidded to a stop behind the rickety structure.

"You leave my dog alone!" the girl's high-pitched voice reached him. "What's the matter with you people?"

Kevin didn't have time to examine his wound. There was nothing else to do but dump the iridium kernel under his tongue before Bill caught him. He spit it out in the dirt, but it wasn't enough. He had to put more distance between him and the kernel, so it would never be found. Ignoring the pain that shot down his right leg, he ran again, straight for the house. He heard the pounding of his pursuers' boots on the packed dirt. Rounding the side of the farmhouse, he saw a rectangular outline in the back door, luckily built for a big dog. He hadn't heard barking when he'd knocked earlier, so hopefully, Fido wasn't home. A glance to the side as he shot through the dog door showed that no one saw him go inside. He skidded to a stop on the wood floor and used his body to stop the dog door from flapping.

He was in a laundry room off the kitchen. Thinking fast, he shapeshifted into the old man and opened the dryer. The doorknob rattled and then a sudden *boom* sounded at the door. Kevin knew he had only seconds before Bill or the soldier kicked it in. There was a load of laundry in the dryer, but it was not, as he'd hoped, full of clothes. Instead, he pulled out a bath towel and slung it around his hips. Then he cranked the sink faucet and dunked his head under, splashing himself thoroughly with water.

When the door burst open, a surprised old man fresh out of the shower confronted the intruders with a querulous, "What d'you lot think yer doin'?"

The hard-faced soldier entered; rifle pointed at Kevin's scrawny, hairless chest. For an authentic look, Kevin had given himself a farmer's tan.

From outside, the girl yelled, "I *found* the clothes! They were in the bloody cave! I never saw anyone and that is *too* my dog!"

Bill came up behind the soldier and tapped him on the shoulder. With a sneer, the man backed out, but he kept his gun trained on Kevin.

"Sorry about that, Mr. Higgins," Bill said. "Did your dog happen to come in just now?"

"Higgins? Are you daft, man?" Kevin asked, with an affronted stare from under bushy brows. Kevin's affinity for languages made it easy to mimic an Irish brogue, but 'aging' his voice put a strain on his vocal cords. "Name's Keane, as you well know. What the bloody hell is this about?"

"Did the dog come in?" Bill repeated, having apparently satisfied himself that Kevin was indeed the real Mr. Keane. Thank goodness Kevin knew the old man's name from the pub waitress, and that he'd gotten a good look at his face when he'd driven by in the old red truck.

Kevin gave a sharp whistle and looked into the kitchen expectantly. After a moment, when no dog made an appearance, he turned and shrugged at Bill. Outwardly, he was all nonchalance, but the pain in his thigh burned relentlessly. He felt a trickle of blood make its way down the back of his leg.

"Whose car is that out front?" Bill asked.

"Rental. Damned lorry broke down again. Now if you don't mind, I'd appreciate it if you'd stop harassing my granddaughter and let me get dressed."

Bill's lips thinned, but after a second, he nodded. "My apologies. As you know, this is a matter of national security. Please discuss the importance of discretion with your granddaughter and remind her to stay away from the mine. Report it to the authorities immediately if either of you have any strange animal sightings or see anyone lurking about."

Kevin adopted what he hoped was a confounded expression. "You mean besides the likes of you and yer goons?" He waved his hand at the door. "Yeah, go on – off with you."

Bill stepped outside and gestured for the girl to give him the bundle of Kevin's clothes. She thrust it into his arms, stomped inside and tried to shut the door. Kevin helped her prop it between the frame on its broken hinges. As soon as it was reasonably in place, she held a finger to her lips and indicated he should follow her. They went through the kitchen, past a living room full of faded, overstuffed furniture, and down a dark hallway. She pointed and he preceded her into a bathroom with chipped and rusty fixtures.

"Yer bleedin' all over the floor," she said quietly. "Let me look at it."

He shook his head and twisted his torso, trying to see the wound without flashing her. In his imitation of her grandfather's voice, he said, "I'm fine. Leave me be."

She grabbed his shoulder and made him look at her. "I know it's you. My grandfather is quite possibly the hairiest man on Earth, and unless he got a full-body wax last time he went into the village, well…you got his face right anyway, but would ya mind, please, switchin' back to your normal self? I don't particularly want to go diggin' for that bullet out of me grandfather's arse, hairy or not."

Kevin couldn't help it; he let out a short laugh. She answered his smile with one of her own. Despite the dark circles under her eyes, it transformed her wan face into one of ethereal beauty. Kevin caught his breath.

Her face slowly sobered. "Let me see it."

He thought she meant the bullet wound, but then she said, "Show me how you change."

"I'd rather not-"

"I'm standin' here in front of you in all my bald-headed glory. If I can reveal myself that way, and after everythin' I've just done for you…"

Suspecting he would lose this and any future argument he might engage in with this feisty young woman, Kevin gave in silently and shapeshifted right then, right in front of her, even though it was something he was wasn't supposed to do – ever. Caitlin was adamant that their very existence depended upon strict discretion, and here he'd gone and blown it ten minutes after encountering this girl.

He knew how it looked; he'd seen Caitlin and Lizbeth shift, and Brian Griffey, the man who'd turned out to be his biological father. He'd

17

seen himself in the mirror many times in the last several months, practicing. The more he did it, the faster and more accurate the change. Going back to his own body was effortless. The girl's mouth dropped open in wonder.

Unfortunately, his body was both shorter and stockier than the old man. As his chest filled out with muscle and his waist expanded from emaciated paunch to flat and firm, the towel around his hips popped open and dropped to the floor.

He snatched at it and missed, bent to pick it up, but the pain in his backside stopped him cold, tearing an agonized expletive from him. To his ultimate humiliation, she retrieved the towel before he could, and, eyes averted, pressed it against his belly. He spun around on the heel of his good leg and said, "There. Do what you gotta do."

He heard water running as she washed her hands and wet down a washcloth. In the mirror over the sink, he watched the top of her hairless head after she knelt down and began gingerly patting the cloth against the wound.

"Oh, good," she said. "I see the entrance wound here," she touched him gently, "and about an inch above that, it looks like the bullet exited straight through this little fatty area at the bottom of your bum."

Kevin felt his face flame. It occurred to him quite suddenly that he had no idea how old this young woman was. She looked like she could be anywhere from fourteen to twenty; like Caitlin, she was very petite. He was about to ask her, when she handed him a roll of medical tape and said, "Tear off four pieces about ten centimeters long, um—what's yer name?"

"Kevin," he mumbled, picking at the tape edge with his fingernail to start it.

"So, are you…a werewolf?"

"No."

"Fairy?"

"I'm human, or I was until the Cataclysm."

He tore off a strip of tape with his teeth, handed it around to her and winced as she pressed a gauze pad in place.

"What happened?" she asked.

He handed her another piece of tape. "Incredibly long and complicated story."

"I've got time. Doc says this round of chemo bought me plenty. Maybe a whole year."

Kevin didn't know what to say to that. He tried to think of some platitude, frustrated as the seconds ticked by without anything coming to him. In desperation, he looked over his shoulder at her and touched her

18

mind. Despite her flippancy, he felt her despair, and it only made it harder for him to respond. Finally, lamely, he turned back around and said, "Well, I don't. I have to get out of here."

She didn't ask any more questions, just finished bandaging his wound. When she washed the blood from the inside of his thigh with the warm washcloth, it sent pleasurable chill bumps sprouting all down his leg.

She stood and dropped the soiled cloth in the sink. "I'll get you some clothes."

"Thanks."

In a few minutes she came back and handed him a pair of plain grey sweatpants and a blue t-shirt.

"These were my grandmother's, but she was rather wider than Grandfather, until the end. His shoes should fit you, though." She left again so he could dress, not that privacy was a big issue at that point.

He found her in the kitchen, a new bandana tied around her head.

Noise from outside alerted them to the helicopter's departure. It seemed to buzz low over the house before fading away.

"Good. They're gone." Kevin started for the door, but she stopped him with a hand on his arm.

"Take me with you."

He looked at her, uncomprehending. "What?"

Her eyes shone with unshed tears. "This is the most amazin' thing that's ever happened to me. No one would ever believe it, not that I would tell. I just—I'd like to help you, whatever it is you're doin'."

Before she even finished speaking, he began to shake his head. She wouldn't be swayed by the 'too dangerous' argument, since she was already dying, so he tried something he'd seen more than once on television, "You'd just get in my way."

He didn't count on her reaction to the blunt statement. She laughed.

"I knew you were goin' to say that. Problem is they took your wallet and the keys to your car. You need me."

"Don't need keys." He held up his hand as if that would explain to her that via some electrical or magnetic action he didn't understand, he could start the engine with a mere touch of his palm.

She didn't try to stop him again, but she did follow him outside. He scanned the area, in case Bill left any of his cohorts behind, but didn't see anyone. With the girl by his side, and at that point he felt it best if he didn't encourage her by asking her name, he limped to the chicken coop.

"Where are you goin'?" she asked.

"Dropped something when I was running before."

"You mean, when you were a dog? What could you have dropped?"

"I had something in my mouth. You need to stay back and be sure not to touch anything. What I'm looking for could kill you."

With evident reluctance, she stopped several yards from the chicken coop.

This time the chickens didn't scatter when he approached; they weren't afraid of humans. A fat brown hen clucked softly as she scratched at the dirt, jabbing her beak at a speck on the ground before moving out of his way. Beyond the chicken coop was a pig pen Kevin hadn't noticed before, and beyond that was what looked like a compost heap, surrounded by a sturdy chicken-wire fence.

"So, what that man was talkin' about, the hazardous something in our mine—is that what you took?" the girl asked. "The thing you don't want me to touch?"

"Yes." He got down on all fours and ran his hand over the dirt. He should be able to sense the biometal kernel, but he felt nothing.

Impossible!

There was no way Bill could have seen him drop the kernel; no way he could have found it in such a short amount of time. Yet after several more minutes of searching, Kevin was forced to admit that the kernel was gone. He didn't think the soldier had been one of the folk; but maybe in all the excitement Kevin had missed the signs. The soldier could have sensed the kernel as he passed by and retrieved it. It was the only answer.

He stood and absentmindedly bent to brush the dirt from his knees, provoking a twinge of pain from his wound.

The sample Bill had taken the first time he'd visited the Keane mine must have contained a minuscule amount of the biometal; otherwise why come back? And now it appeared Kevin had provided him with the rest of it. With the kernel in his possession, Bill would be a very dangerous man. His single-minded attempts in the past to become a shapeshifter like his beloved Caitlin had inadvertently set the Gossamer Sphere in motion in the first place, unleashing the horrible destruction of the Cataclysm on the world.

Bill understood that only descendants of the folk could survive contact with the biometal. It activated a code for shapeshifting characteristics hidden in the DNA of all mammals and changed them, just as Kevin and Lizbeth had been changed. Bill knew that not all initiates survived the change, but what he didn't know was how the very first shapeshifters had survived. If he figured out how the biometal could change non-descendants, he would not only have found what he'd been so desperately seeking; he would be giving whatever government or paramilitary group he was working with the power to create an army of shapeshifters.

Kevin had to warn Caitlin. He straightened and broke into a limping run towards his rental car. After he passed her, the girl said loudly, *"Tara!"*

He slowed up a bit and looked around.

"My name," she said, offering him a rueful smile.

He opened the car door and lifted his hand. "Thanks, Tara. Good luck."

Chapter Five

Baltimore, Maryland

Lizbeth wasn't very good at reading minds yet, but after Indira accused Caitlin of having an ulterior motive for her visit, it seemed like a good time to practice. She reached out with her gossamers, the waves of magnetic energy produced by electrical activity in her brain, and tentatively connected with Indira's mind.

Caitlin crossed her arms and gave Indira a look of fond exasperation. "You've gotten cynical. What else would I be here for?"

Indira's thoughts were jumbled, but Lizbeth picked up an image of a large metal box, a machine of some sort, and flashes of the starry sky where three stars in a row seemed to be getting brighter.

"That depends on who you work for," Indira replied.

"I'm unemployed at the moment," Caitlin said slowly. "What's going on?"

Indira produced a laugh that sounded forced and took a few steps back. "A lot, actually. Look, I have a lecture, but a bunch of us are meeting at The Cosmos at five. Stop by and have a drink. We'll talk more, okay?"

"Will Sam be there?"

Indira gave her a half-nod. "And I'm sure he'll be interested to find out what you've been up to. I'll see you later, then?"

"Yes, certainly."

Indira turned towards the Muller building and Caitlin and Lizbeth went in the opposite direction towards the parking lot, across a sweeping expanse of grass still brown from the lingering winter.

"Did you read her?" Caitlin asked.

"I didn't pick up much. Just a machine and a star."

"I got that, too. Some kind of an electrical device. The star... I don't think that's what Indira thought it was."

Caitlin's cell phone rang with a burst of bagpipes that was cut off before Lizbeth could discern any particular tune, if there was one. She listened to Caitlin's side of the conversation.

"Hello? Have you found it?"

Whatever the caller said, it made Caitlin drift to a stop unknowingly right in the middle of a patch of melting snow.

"Are you certain?"

At the urgent tone, Lizbeth began to get alarmed. When Caitlin's jaw clenched and her brows dropped like thunderclouds, Lizbeth felt a cold rush of fear. Whatever the caller said must be serious if it upset the unflappable Caitlin.

"Ditch the car, the phone, everything. Get to my Dublin box, and only call me at this number on a secure phone if it's an emergency. Wait for us at the place we discussed. We'll be there tomorrow night or the day after at the latest." She listened for a moment, then rang off and began walking at such a rapid pace that Lizbeth, whose legs were only slightly longer than her grandmother's, had difficulty keeping up.

"What's wrong?"

"That was Kevin. He found the original biometal cache and mined what remained into a conveniently sized bit for Bill to steal from him. *Damn it!* I should have gone to see him. This wouldn't have happened if I'd just soothed his injured pride."

Lizbeth knew the "him" in Caitlin's rant was Bill Masters, Caitlin's former lover – and a resourceful man who knew all about the folk. They couldn't afford to have him working for the other side – the other side being just about everyone who wasn't a shapeshifter, but particularly those who could potentially profit from the knowledge that shapeshifters really existed. Like the British government or the Guild, a mysterious and fanatical group whose sole purpose since the Inquisition was to capture, torture and kill the folk.

They got into the rental car and Lizbeth looked out over the peaceful campus while Caitlin called the airline and began negotiating for a couple of seats to London.

Caitlin, as the last of the ancient druid nobility, had a duty to protect her people, to guard the gossamer crown from those who would steal its secrets. Now that Bill Masters had a sample of the biometal the crown had been forged from, Caitlin would have to bring together all her resources to stop him – again.

Once the call concluded, Caitlin said, "We're on standby for tomorrow morning, but I'm afraid the chance of getting a flight is slim. We may have to waylay a few passengers and assume their identities to get on board."

Lizbeth tried to keep her apprehension from showing. "Why don't we get a charter flight like we did before?"

"It's impossible to get a last-minute charter nowadays. Too many planes went down in the Cataclysm. Don't look at me like that. I'm not suggesting we kill anyone."

Lizbeth hadn't thought she was. She just didn't think 'waylaying' someone sounded all that safe, or for that matter, like something she was even capable of doing. She had to remind herself that Caitlin probably did stuff like that all the time.

They checked into their hotel and once they got up to the room, Caitlin unzipped her suitcase and rummaged inside.

"Here." She tossed Lizbeth a long-sleeved white turtleneck followed by a sleeveless blue cardigan, a black skirt and some black tights.

"Um," Lizbeth began.

"Put those on."

"Right. So, why again are we masquerading as nuns?"

Caitlin unzipped a garment bag and removed a burgundy sweater with a deep rounded neckline. She turned her blue eyes on Lizbeth and twitched the sweater on its hanger. "Does this look like a nun's habit? No, my dear, we're going to meet Indira at the bar. You are underage, and we don't have time to fudge an ID for you, therefore you must appear to be significantly older than you are so you don't get carded."

"How significantly?" Lizbeth asked in a weak voice.

"Can you do Annette?"

Lizbeth had never attempted to shift into her other grandmother's face, but she certainly couldn't pull off Annette Moreau's bulk. Adding the breasts alone would require borrowing several inches from her height.

"Not unless you want me to be two feet tall."

Caitlin laughed, a rare occurrence. "Well, pick someone else, then."

Other than an assortment of actresses and a few teachers back in high school, none of whom Lizbeth wanted to emulate, she didn't know a lot of old women. Then she thought of someone and shifted.

"How about this?"

Caitlin, in the process of removing her travel clothes, turned. A smile blossomed. "Perfect. We won't have to invent a name I might forget."

Later, when they walked into The Cosmos, Lizbeth wrinkled Felicity's nose and said in her best imitation of an elderly Irish lady, "It smells like sour whiskey and vomit in here."

24

No one heard her pronouncement over the piped-in music; a loud, monotonous techno that seemed more suited to a night club than a bar, not that Lizbeth had ever been to either.

She swept her gaze around the sprawling space. At the center was a round, white Formica bar that looked retro, but as they got closer the chipped surface and cigarette burns from days gone by suggested it was original from the 1980's or earlier. The theme, not surprisingly for a place called "The Cosmos," was an astrological mishmash. The ceiling was painted black with contrasting speckles that were supposed to represent the night sky. The walls had framed mug shots of astronauts, photos of the moon landing and various planets, nebula and quite a few pictures of the surface of Mars.

Against the walls were booths upholstered in red vinyl. Low sofas with coffee tables occupied the rest of the space. The Cosmos was packed with people; they overflowed from the booths, sat on the arms of the couches, and stood four-deep around the bar, like ants waiting their turn at a drop of honey on the kitchen counter. The hum of conversation competed with the techno music.

"There they are," Caitlin said near Lizbeth's ear. "Don't talk much and follow my lead. These people may be drinking, but they're all brilliant."

From a booth near the back, Indira half-stood and waved them over. Heavy glass mugs and plastic pitchers of beer, mostly empty, littered the table. There were six people crammed together, three men and three women, including Indira. Caitlin seemed to know them all, and Lizbeth stood silently as she said her hellos, complete with hugs and laughter.

"This is my aunt Felicity," Caitlin said.

"Oh, from Ireland, right?" Indira asked. "Caitlin spoke of you often."

Suddenly in the spotlight, Lizbeth panicked. She'd been planning to use her normal voice, but now that she'd been outed as an Irishwoman, she'd have to use Felicity's distinctive lilt, which she wasn't sure she could mimic well enough to fool anyone, much less a table full of "brilliant" scientists. What if one of them questioned her about Ireland? Other than a vague notion of what St. Patrick's Day was all about, she knew exactly bupkis about the country.

The expectant smiles were beginning to fade by the time Lizbeth chose not to speak at all. She grinned foolishly and nodded her head in a bobbing motion that loosened a lock of Felicity's white hair from its demure bun. She turned away from the others, ostensibly to tuck the stray lock back into place. The moment passed, and it seemed as if Caitlin's old friends would be content to ignore the dotty elderly lady.

A pudgy man with Benjamin Franklin spectacles insisted Lizbeth take his seat in the booth. He scrounged up two chairs, placing them at the end of the table and partially blocking the aisle. Caitlin sat in one of the chairs and he sat next to her.

The topic of conversation before they arrived had apparently been the Cataclysm. The pudgy man, who Lizbeth eventually identified as Sam, sat quietly as another man launched into his theory of how the earthquakes, volcanism and magnetic field anomalies were related. A woman laughingly countered with a theory of her own. A good-natured argument ensued, but Lizbeth noticed Indira and Sam stayed silent. Finally, a mousy woman in the corner asked, "What do you think caused it, Caitlin?"

After a brief pause, Caitlin replied in a serious tone, "Due to the many indignities the human race has heaped upon the earth in the last century, I think the planet was attempting to eradicate the infestation."

Everyone at the table burst out laughing, but Lizbeth didn't even crack a smile, since Caitlin's comment was uncomfortably close to the truth.

Sam held up his beer mug and squinted at the dregs. "Our waitress must have noticed the insignia on Indira's shirt and figured us astronomy types for bad tippers."

"Well, historically it's been true," Indira said mildly. "Why don't you get us another pitcher at the bar? I have to hit the restroom."

She stood and Lizbeth saw Caitlin reach out and pull Indira's long black coat off the bench into her lap. For the first time, Lizbeth noticed her grandmother was dressed in the same colors as Indira. Caitlin touched her arm and sent: *Follow her and keep her in the restroom. Give me ten minutes.*

Lizbeth immediately stood.

"Oh, Aunt Felicity," Caitlin said, regret in her voice. "I forgot your medication. I'll go out to the car to get it and then stop at the bar for a glass of water."

"Thank you, dear. I'll just pop into the ladies." Lizbeth was mortified to hear her voice come out sounding like a bad Julia Child imitation, but luckily nobody seemed to notice.

In the bathroom, she went straight to the mirror over the row of sinks in the restroom, wondering how she was supposed to delay Indira for ten whole minutes. The toilet in the stall behind her flushed. Thinking fast, she turned on the faucet, cupped her hands to fill them with water, and dumped it down her front. A dark wet spot appeared in the center of the blue cardigan. She pulled a fistful of paper towels out of the dispenser just as Indira exited the stall.

"Oh, hello, Felicity. What happened?"

Lizbeth made a show of dabbing at herself ineffectually. "A very rude young man, and I must assume he was pissed out of his mind – excuse me – I mean to say he was drunk, spilled his lager all over me without the slightest effort at apology."

Indira looked sympathetic but didn't seem to be inclined to help Lizbeth blot the stain – forgivable considering it was located across her chest and abdomen. Indira washed and dried her hands and just when Lizbeth came to the conclusion she was going to have to fake a heart attack to keep her in the bathroom, Indira said, "Your accent is…interesting."

In her head, Lizbeth produced a Homer Simpson, "D'Oh!"

But she relaxed as Indira continued, "It sounds as if you've been in the states for some time."

"Eighteen years now," Lizbeth said, which, given her actual age, was true.

"I put a lot of effort after I emigrated into losing my accent," Indira said. "Every once in a while, it slips out, though, usually when I'm angry."

When all else fails, Lizbeth thought, get them talking about themselves. "Where are you from?"

She spent the next little while nodding her head, eyes fixed on Indira's as if she were enraptured with every word the Indian woman said, tossing out a question now and then to keep her talking. She wasn't able to occupy her for more than five minutes, however, since Indira quite suddenly interrupted herself to say, "Listen to me, going on like that. I need to get back out there before Happy Hour is over."

Lizbeth hurried after her, scanning the vicinity for Caitlin. She didn't see her grandmother anywhere, but she *did* notice another Indira at the bar, wrapped in her black overcoat and talking earnestly to Sam.

The real Indira was just ahead of her, not yet within line of sight of their booth. Thinking fast, Lizbeth stepped up alongside her and deliberately stumbled, knocking the surprised woman sideways into the table at another booth. The couple at the table grabbed for their glasses to keep them from overturning, but beer sloshed over their hands onto the tabletop. As Indira helped the couple wipe up the mess, Lizbeth stood there flapping her hands, saying, "I'm so sorry," to no one in particular.

Once the spilled beer was cleaned up, Indira murmured apologies to the couple and turned to Lizbeth, holding a mass of sopping napkins in one hand. Lizbeth blocked her way, stuttering a rambling excuse about weak ankles and bad eyesight. When it looked like Indira had reached the limit of polite tolerance, Lizbeth glanced over her shoulder and saw Sam making his way back to their booth with a pitcher in his hand. Caitlin – or the other Indira – was nowhere in sight.

Lizbeth stepped aside and let Indira pass, following her timidly back to the table. Caitlin appeared from behind, placing a hand on Lizbeth's shoulder. "Are you alright, Aunt Felicity?" Then she sent: *Take the coat*, and Lizbeth put her hands behind her so Caitlin could pass Indira's coat to her.

"Need my medicine," Lizbeth muttered, trying to look sick and distressed.

Caitlin shook her head. "I'm afraid we've left it at the hotel." To the group, she said, "It was wonderful seeing you all again. So sorry we have to cut this short, but her dosage schedule is crucial."

As everyone offered their goodbyes, Lizbeth stood there with no idea what to do with the coat. There was no way even an accomplished pickpocket such as herself could get the coat into the booth without being seen. So she did the only thing she could think of: while Caitlin gathered their coats and purses, she glanced around to make sure no one was looking and dropped it on the floor. Someone would pick it up eventually.

Soon they were speeding down the highway towards the safety of the hotel. Lizbeth's heart was still thumping so hard she wished she really did have some medicine waiting for her in the room. She crossed her fingers that they would get a flight on standby the next day, so they didn't have to "waylay" anyone. This was not as easy as Caitlin made it look.

Chapter Six

San Francisco, California

"The Ritz again, huh?" Zach asked. The London Ritz had been where Zach met Seamus during the height of the Cataclysm. It was lunchtime, the day after Seamus revealed he'd been masquerading as H.Q. Spencer for the last seven decades.

"I always stay at the Ritz," Seamus replied. He was H.Q. today, complete with corduroy jacket with the obligatory patches on the elbows, an old pair of chinos and tasseled loafers.

Zach looked around the foyer, mentally comparing the two hotels. He'd never seen the inside of the San Francisco Ritz before the Cataclysm, but it was just as opulent as its London counterpart, even though the marble flooring was zig-zagged with cracks that the guests, accustomed to the uneven ground all over the city, stepped over nonchalantly.

The buildings downtown that hadn't been reduced to rubble had not been left untouched by the earthquakes, and the Ritz-Carlton was no exception. The topmost floors were off-limits and familiar red and yellow building inspector tags fluttered everywhere. The façade, formerly a grand, roman-style colonnade, had been laid bare. But the iconic building still stood and was therefore occupied. Much of the city had burned, but the crooked buildings that had survived had not been abandoned; on the contrary. Tens of thousands of remaining displaced people had to live somewhere, and those who could work had been industriously rebuilding for the last nine months. The building inspector tags were a mere formality, ignored by all. It was common knowledge safety could not be guaranteed. There was no place for personal injury lawsuits in the post-Cataclysm cities of the American west coast.

Zach made brief eye contact with an armed security guard, one of three he'd seen since he'd arrived. Martial law was still in effect in some parts of the Bay Area, but not here. It was not exactly business as usual, but people from all over the world still had reason to visit and needed places to stay, so hotels like the Ritz were open, staffed, and guarded.

While they waited to be seated in the hotel lounge, Seamus asked, "You know who Arthur Davis was?" At Zach's headshake, Seamus said, "He was one of the architects for the London Ritz. I served with him in World War I."

This casual declaration from a man who normally looked no older than thirty-five didn't faze Zach. Seamus was a full shapeshifter like Caitlin, and just as old. Caitlin had been shocked to discover so many of the folk had survived. After the Roman slaughter and then later, the Inquisition, when so many had perished at the hands of the Guild, she thought there were only a handful left. She'd kept track of those she knew about, and their descendants, like Zach. Then the Cataclysm brought more of them out of hiding. Seamus had been instrumental in gathering them together to lend their strength to Caitlin, the legendary Last Noble.

"Art had brilliant ideas but was none too stable." Seamus rotated his index finger in a circle next to his temple.

After the hostess seated them at a window table that overlooked a great pile of debris, Zach studied the menu. The prices, which had undoubtedly been high before it became nearly impossible to get good food, were outrageous. H.Q. Spencer was rich though, so Zach didn't feel the slightest pang ordering a seventy-dollar hamburger and fries. He hadn't had the quintessential American meal in so long his mouth began watering before he could take the first bite.

"So how am I supposed to help you fake H.Q.'s death?" he asked around a mouthful of wonderful.

"Simple. Come to my one-hundredth birthday party. It's tonight. I've chartered a ferryboat."

"And…?"

"Well, as I said, I created an heir for H.Q. recently. Someone young and dashing that he could leave all his money to. You come with me tonight and pose as that heir, and I'll take a nosedive off the deck in front of a load of witnesses. I'll change into a sea lion, swim to shore and we can trade places at a predetermined time and place. Then I'll become my heir again, shed a few crocodile tears over H.Q.'s empty casket and voilà."

"Sounds great, except…you do know I'm not a shapeshifter, right? How am I supposed to pose as your…" he drifted off and stared at Seamus, suddenly suspicious.

The bard raised a hand in a calming gesture. "I did borrow your likeness to create Dawson, but—" he raised his voice and spoke rapidly over Zach's protest, "I'll make it worth your while!"

Zach leaned back in his chair, wiping juicy burger drippings from between his fingers with the restaurant's stiff cloth napkin. "It would have been nice if you'd asked first."

Seamus hardly looked contrite. "I know, and I considered it, but then I figured you'd be grateful for the money."

It was true. Zach's family was in dire straits. "How much money?"

Seamus pressed H.Q.'s thin lips together and tilted his head as if he hadn't considered an actual amount. He shrugged and said casually, "Ten thousand?"

Zach had just taken a sip of his soda, another luxury he sorely missed, and his gasp sent the liquid down the wrong pipe. He choked and then coughed for so long Seamus got up, shuffled slowly around the table and patted him lightly on the back. Zach waved him away as the spasms receded. When he could finally talk, he said, "For that much, I'll be anyone you want me to be."

"Fabulous. The party's tonight. I'll pick you up at four. Don't bother dressing; I'll bring your outfit. Oh, and here," Seamus pulled a sheaf of folded papers from his pocket. "Memorize this. You'll need to know who you're pretending to be."

Chapter Seven

Dublin, Ireland

After calling Caitlin, Kevin didn't bother going back to his hotel. His wallet, complete with ID, credit card and cash, not to mention the keycard to his room, was now in Bill Masters' possession. His passport and clothes were in the hotel room, but Caitlin had told him to ditch everything and pick up a new identity from the nearest box. He'd known before he left the states that it was a risk for him to travel under his real name, but all of Caitlin's pre-established identities were female and he flat out hated to assume a body so foreign to his nature.

Now he had no choice, of course. He was planning to do a partial, a female face and upper body, while the rest of him stayed, as his mother would put it, "As God intended."

He carefully chose a side road outside of Dublin, where he parked and shapeshifted into someone who didn't look out of place in Tara's grandmother's sweatpants and t-shirt. Looking exactly like the nondescript man in his fifties he'd sat next to on the plane three weeks ago, he left the rental car and speed-walked for about a kilometer, pumping his arms, elbows high. The brisk exercise was not intended as an attempt to stay in character so much as to keep warm in the chill afternoon. His destination was a small post office, one of many all over the world Caitlin used, where she rented out boxes in which she stashed whatever she would need to quickly assume a new identity.

It had just begun drizzling when he entered the shop, empty but for the elderly man behind the cash register, who called out, "We've got a nice shipment of umbrellas, there by the door."

Kevin glanced at a display hung with brightly colored umbrellas and lifted a hand in acknowledgement. He weaved his way through shelves of greeting cards and knickknacks to the back of the store, where the rental

32

boxes occupied an entire wall. It took him a few minutes to remember the number of Caitlin's box, but she used the same combination on all her locks, so once located, he had no trouble opening it. He removed the contents, a magazine-sized envelope, and headed for the exit.

"Whoa there, friend," the old man said. He'd come out from behind the counter and was blocking Kevin's way. "I'm the proprietor. Box 12A, was it?"

Kevin narrowed his eyes. "What's it to you?"

The proprietor shrugged. "That box has been mostly untouched for seven years. You might be interested to know the police were 'round a few weeks ago asking about it."

Kevin tried to hide his shock. "Asking what?"

"Fact is they had a look inside. I overheard them whilst they were counting your euros. Be happy to tell you what the discussion was about...for a price."

All of Caitlin's boxes had the same amount of money in them. Kevin knew the envelope in his hand had five hundred twenty-euro notes in it. From the sound of it, the proprietor was also privy to that information.

He sighed. "How much?"

The proprietor lifted his bushy white eyebrows. "Coppers told me I'd get a substantial reward for calling them were the box owner to show up."

Kevin opened the envelope and dug through the contents until he found a smaller envelope. From the thickness, he figured it was the money. He pulled it out and began thumbing through the crisp notes inside. "What guarantee can you give me that you won't take my money and call them anyway?"

The proprietor lifted his chin and produced an offended sniff. "I give you my word, and that's not given lightly. Besides, if you don't want them to find you, you'd be well advised to hear what I've got to say."

As if weighing his options, Kevin put a contemplative look on his face and gazed into the old man's rheumy blue eyes; all the while, he was reaching out with his gossamers. Within seconds, he'd plucked the information he needed from the forefront of the proprietor's mind. He looked back into the large envelope. The GPS tracking device was smaller than he expected, about the size of a thick credit card. It wasn't cleverly hidden, but its plastic housing was the same orangey-dun color as the envelope, and it was attached with some kind of double-stick tape to the side near the bottom. The police had assumed rightly that he would have taken the entire envelope with him without finding it, giving them time to follow and catch him.

After reading the proprietor's mind, he knew the old codger had every intention of taking his money *and* calling the police. The proprietor felt justified invoking the old 'my word is my bond' chestnut because he honestly felt it didn't apply to criminals, which he assumed Kevin was.

If Caitlin were here, Kevin had a feeling she'd have already overpowered or outsmarted the old guy and tied him up in the back room or something, but since Kevin was a newbie at this game, he wasn't about to attempt anything physical.

Subterfuge was more his style. He met the old man's eyes again, reached out with his gossamers, and said, "If you call the police, I'll tell them about that secret you've been hiding...Mr. Parker."

Kevin was just fishing, hoping to pick up on something he could use to influence the old man. The last thing he expected was to reel in a whopper. While the proprietor blustered, "What's that supposed to mean? I'm a law-abiding citizen," Kevin caught a flash of panic, followed by a quick succession of dark memories: a gunshot, a corpse, an unmarked grave.

Mr. Parker turned and took one step towards the counter, but stopped when Kevin said quietly, "You think there's much left of Charlie after forty years in the ground?"

Other than the convulsive bobbing of Mr. Parker's Adam's apple as he silently choked on his fear, he didn't move.

"How did you know?" he finally whispered.

"Doesn't matter. Just don't call the cops."

Mr. Parker nodded. With barely moving lips, he said, "Wouldn't dream of it."

Kevin didn't bother to read his mind again. It was patently obvious Mr. Parker would now keep his word.

Kevin kept the cash but set the larger envelope on a shelf on top of some decorative candles. The new identity was useless to him now. The police would certainly have made note of it. He was almost glad he didn't have to become a woman.

Mr. Parker still stood facing away from him as he headed for the door. The old man didn't see him lift a green umbrella from its display hook as he went out into the rainy afternoon.

Chapter Eight

Baltimore, Maryland

It had taken hours for Lizbeth to fall asleep in the unfamiliar bed, so when the harsh sound of bagpipes from Caitlin's ringtone intruded on her slumber, she rolled over and pulled a pillow over her head, holding it pressed to her ear. She hoped she'd be able to slip back into sleep, but a hand shook her shoulder. She groaned in protest and Caitlin left her alone long enough for her to doze back off, but then the heavy coverlet was suddenly yanked down.

"Get up. We need to go."

When Lizbeth didn't respond, Caitlin tugged the pillow out from under her arm and said sternly, "*Now.*"

Lizbeth rolled over and squinted at the display on the clock radio. "It's four in the morning!"

"Yes, it is." Caitlin must have gotten dressed while Lizbeth was stealing a few more precious minutes of sleep, because she was wearing dark jeans and a black shirt. She went over to Lizbeth's open suitcase and began rummaging through her clothes. She pulled out a pair of jeans, a dark green sweater and Lizbeth's low-heeled boots and tossed them on the foot of the bed. "Put these on. Make haste."

Lizbeth sat up groggily, yawned and slid her legs off the side of the bed. "Who was on the phone? Kevin?"

"Yes. Get dressed."

Lizbeth stood and stripped off her pajama top. "What's wrong?"

Caitlin was sorting through her own things now and stuffing items into a black leather satchel, but she paused for a moment and regarded Lizbeth with serious blue eyes. "He went to my box outside of Dublin and discovered that the police had already been there. They put a tracking device in the envelope with the identity papers."

As Lizbeth pulled on her jeans and reached for the sweater, she thought back to Simon's isolated, rundown farm, and the murders that had occurred there. The police in England had been unable to solve those crimes, and had also been unable to locate their missing Chief Inspector. They would never know that the one dead man they'd been unable to identify *was* their Chief Inspector, Brian Griffey. They'd scrutinized Caitlin but had been unable to add homicide to the charge of escaping jail. Then she'd gone and escaped again, which probably put her high up on some Most Wanted list or another.

"Is there still a warrant out for you?"

"I'm sure there is," Caitlin replied. "But I don't think that has anything to do with it. I rented the Dublin box with an assumed name years ago. Connecting that name with me would take resources the locals just don't have. This is the work of the Guild, or worse, an agency like MI6. Until I learn otherwise, I must assume all of my boxes, and therefore all of the identities I've compiled, have somehow been compromised."

"Even the ones we're travelling under now?"

Caitlin sat on the bed and rested her elbows on her knees, looking up at Lizbeth soberly. "There's something I should tell you. The reason I came to get you for this trip was not just to get to know you, although that's been very nice."

Lizbeth smiled and waited.

"I'm afraid there've been some...complications that will make it impossible for you to resume your former life."

"What do you mean?" Lizbeth asked weakly.

"Last month I was in Philadelphia, where a covert group of supposedly British agents detained Seamus in an attempt to coerce me to give them the crown."

"British agents in the US?"

"Yes. Seamus got the impression they were not working in concert with their American counterparts, but he had no way to know for certain since some of the agents sounded like locals."

Lizbeth frowned. "How did they find him?"

"They interviewed the crew of the drill ship, one of whom told them about a teenage girl named Tainie, one of the folk who aided us in stopping the Gossamer Sphere. Apparently Tainie's mother didn't know enough not to reveal anything about themselves and mentioned they were from Philadelphia. These agents went to great lengths to find her. She's related to Seamus on her mother's side, and Brian Griffey is apparently her father."

36

"Oh," Lizbeth said softly. That would make Tainie Kevin's half-sister. "Does Kevin know?"

"I told him, yes, but none of that is relevant to this discussion." Caitlin had fallen back on the severe tone she'd used when they first met. "The point of my telling you this is that you understand how essential it is for us to stay as far under the radar as possible. I want you to promise not to contact your mother without my knowing."

Lizbeth hesitated. Her mother had tried to convince her not to use her abilities, and a rift had formed between them when Lizbeth had obstinately refused. When Caitlin appeared on their doorstep in Cataclysm-torn Alaska, it had taken every ounce of persuasiveness to convince her mother to let her go. Despite the fact that she'd just turned eighteen and could do as she pleased, Lizbeth didn't want to leave on bad terms.

"I'll be able to call her sometime, though, right?"

Caitlin sighed. "Under controlled circumstances we can get a message to her, but keep in mind if they were willing to use Seamus to get to me, they'll use anyone."

"So...she's in danger?"

"Always. Why do you think she disappeared with you in the first place? Anyone associated with us is at risk. It has been thus for centuries. The Guild has penetrated and influenced organizations from the Catholic Church to the Nazi Party, but they are no longer all we need to fear. The Guild used religion and superstition to gain leverage. One might suppose we'd be safer from persecution now, that it would be more difficult for them to gain support against us."

"But now we're up against science."

"Exactly. When those scientists on the drill ship died after coming into contact with the biometal..."

"It opened a bag of Gummy Worms." It was one of her granma's favorite sayings.

Caitlin nodded. "Nothing kicks scientific investigation into gear faster than a deadly mystery. These British agents, Lizbeth, went to a lot of trouble to get evidence against us. They compiled a list of names that has you, me, Seamus, Kevin and Zach on it, among others. When they caught Seamus, they tricked him into shifting – all on a live feed to their headquarters. They know what we are."

"So...is it safe for us to get on the plane?"

Caitlin sighed. "There's no such thing as 'safe' for us. And no, we won't be able to travel under the names we've been using. If they uncovered one of my identities, they may have found others."

Lizbeth stuffed her pajamas into her suitcase and zipped it up, but Caitlin said, "Don't bother. We'll be travelling light. Take only the necessities you can carry in your purse."

Lizbeth looked down at the suitcase she'd borrowed from her mother. "You mean, just leave all my stuff here?"

"Yes. Be sure to remove and destroy anything that might identify you, like that tag attached to your luggage with your mother's name and address on it."

Obediently, Lizbeth removed the tag. "What about fingerprints?"

"What do you mean? Didn't you erase yours like I showed you?"

Lizbeth gestured to the suitcase. "I meant my mom's."

Caitlin winced. "Bring it along. We'll ditch it on the way to the airport. I'll replace your things when circumstances allow."

Lizbeth didn't ask when that was likely to be. Her life was no longer on a parallel path to that of the average teen, but it appeared she didn't have time to contemplate what that might mean. She shrugged into her jacket.

"Why do I have the feeling we're about to 'waylay' someone?"

Caitlin smiled enigmatically and chucked Lizbeth lightly under the chin. "Because you're a very bright girl. Let's go."

Chapter Nine

San Francisco, California

Zach leaned casually against the deck rail and tried not to stare as an actress he'd had a crush on since the sixth grade paraded by with her retinue. She stopped to point at the antenna array over the helm, laughing at the unusual sight of a raven watching over the party. Zach was used to having Caw follow him everywhere, but even he was surprised the bird had come aboard the chartered ferryboat. He suspected Caw was drawn to Seamus, a full shapeshifter whose power the bird probably sensed somehow.

Seamus, in his guise as the normally reclusive H.Q. Spencer, sat next to Zach in a chair by the railing. He was nursing a glass of champagne and smiling beatifically, expertly playing the part of genial, borderline senile old man. He told the same joke to everyone he spoke with, a completely unfunny and slightly racist story about why his nephew was Asian.

They were on the top deck, three levels up from the water. Seamus had failed to mention that the majority of his hundred- and fifty-party guests were either famous, semi-famous, or infamous. Zach had been beating down his fan boy urges all evening, as H.Q.'s high-profile friends stopped by one by one to wish him well. Each of them was introduced to Zach, who did his best to act like the heir to a multi-millionaire.

A prominent movie director had just moved off when Seamus leaned close and said, "You're laying it on a bit thick. Could you try not to come across as so phony?"

"Phony? Really? I was going for unimpressed, which hasn't been easy."

"Well, if you're planning on becoming an initiate, I suggest you bone up on your acting skills. Shifting requires more than what's on the outside."

Zach lifted his eyebrows and looked out over the black water. The lights of the San Francisco skyline were radically different now. Not all of the skyscrapers that were still standing had power, so there were whole sections that were dark. "Not sure I'm going to get the chance. Caitlin's dead set against letting anyone else take the risk."

"She might not have a choice. Things are different now."

Zach wasn't sure if he meant different because Bill Masters was determined to expose them or because the Gossamer Sphere had revealed the presence of an alien race somewhere out in the universe. Maybe he meant both. Zach was just about to ask him, when Seamus said quietly, "Now's a good time. No one's standing close enough to stop me. Walk away."

Zach took a deep breath and nodded. He turned his back and had taken four steps when he heard a woman say, "H.Q! Be careful!" Zach was supposed to keep walking, but he couldn't very well ignore the woman's warning. He spun around and saw that Seamus had stepped up on the chair. The 'old man' was woozily holding his champagne glass aloft, as if he were about to make a toast. There were maybe twenty people on deck, but before any of them could react, he toppled backwards over the rail.

A collective gasp rose from the witnesses and more than one woman screamed. On cue, Zach rushed to the nearest life preserver and snatched it from its hook. "Get out of the way!" he shouted, pushing through the people who'd crowded the rail to look for H.Q. in the water.

The lights shining through the lower deck windows reflected on the inky black surface, but otherwise, he saw nothing. The boat had been maintaining a leisurely pace, but even as he hurled the foam ring over the rail, he detected that it was slowing down.

"Someone jump in and get him!" a woman shouted.

"It's too far down and the water's freezing," a man countered. "It'd be suicide."

"But he'll die!"

Zach felt the stares as people looked to 'Dawson' to rescue his 'uncle.' He said miserably, "I can't swim."

It wasn't true, but he and Seamus had planned for him to say it, planned for him to stand there helplessly and let H.Q. 'drown.' They would never find the body, of course, but with this many witnesses, Dawson would be blameless.

Just then, Caw flew down and landed on Zach's shoulder. It wasn't uncommon for the bird to do so, but it *was* strange that he began to squawk loudly, something he only did to sound the alarm when something was wrong. Over the nine months since the cataclysm, Zach had come to rely on Caw in many ways. The bird was uncannily smart and knew things a mere

40

bird should not know. Zach looked into Caw's blue eyes and tried to send the mental message that Seamus was okay. What he didn't expect was to get a clear impression back from the bird that everything was most definitely *not* okay.

"Something's wrong," he muttered, yanking off the borrowed tuxedo jacket and sending Caw flying. He toed off his shoes and climbed onto the chair. Just before he launched himself out over the water, he heard someone say, "I thought you couldn't swim!"

Zach hit the water feet first, shooting downward in a cold black abyss that reminded him of the last time he'd been submerged in an ocean. He and Lizbeth had been swept overboard by the plume of water from a satellite knocked from the sky. He'd forgotten how painful the cold water was; when he came up for air, the spasming muscles of his diaphragm almost refused to function. Breathing, normally an unconscious action, became an effort.

A glance showed the ferry stalled about a hundred yards away. A boat was being lowered over the side. Caw hovered in the air nearby, squawking madly. Zach took a breath and swam towards the bird as fast as his leaden arms and legs would allow. He expected to find nothing; expected Seamus to have sunk to the bottom of the bay by now, but he found him, floating face-down. He grasped a handful of his hair with one hand and managed to turn him onto his back. Tucking his forearm under Seamus' chin, Zach frog kicked backwards.

He heard a motor come to life somewhere behind him and shouted, "Hey!" A light passed over him, and then came swiftly back to spotlight his progress. He stopped trying to haul Seamus along at that point and focused instead on staying afloat – and keeping Seamus' head above water, even though he wasn't sure he was breathing.

It wasn't until the inflatable dinghy, with its bright portable light, pulled up alongside them that he realized Seamus looked like himself again. A shapeshifter would retain whatever shape they'd taken even when asleep, but when dead, they reverted to their original form.

Fearful Seamus had died, Zach got a burst of adrenaline that fueled his flagging energy. His high school water polo days came back to him as his legs instinctively churned out a strong eggbeater kick that propelled him upward so he could wrap an arm around the cylindrical side of the boat. The two rescuers reached for Seamus and hauled his limp body aboard, then helped Zach out of the water.

41

Zach expected the men to question him when they saw Seamus' face, but they didn't. He realized neither man had actually seen or knew who'd gone into the water.

One of the men checked Seamus' vitals and said, "I got a pulse, but he's in respiratory arrest." He set a CPR mask over Seamus' face and began rescue breaths as the other man piloted the boat towards the ferry.

It was at that moment that Zach noticed one of Seamus' jacket sleeves was empty. He was missing his left arm. Had it been severed when he fell overboard? Had Seamus been sucked under the ferry and chopped up by the propeller? Zach reached out but didn't touch anything as it occurred to him that if the arm had been cut off, the sleeve, too, would be gone.

Zach's entire body went into violent shivers. His worry for Seamus overshadowed everything, but in the back of his mind, he was also concerned that Seamus' careful plan was now ruined. Even if the one-armed shapeshifter regained consciousness, he couldn't very well become H.Q. Spencer now that the rescuers had seen his real face. The jig, as they say, was well and truly up.

Chapter Ten

County Wicklow, Ireland

The last place Kevin expected to find himself after yesterday's fiasco losing the biometal kernel was back at old man Keane's farm, but here he was in the driveway, sitting in a stolen car.

Not long after leaving the post office, he'd shifted into a new face in case the proprietor had a change of heart. He had no doubt a security camera had captured his real image, so he gave himself the face of an old classmate. Then he'd made his way to a department store, where he used Caitlin's euros to purchase three sets of clothes, a good winter coat, a decent pair of boots, and a backpack. After a quick trip to a corner drugstore to get fresh bandages and ointment for his gunshot wound, he'd checked into a cheap hostel that turned out to be clean, but noisy.

He slept lightly and woke hungry. It was during breakfast at a nearby coffee shop that he had the epiphany.

The world's food shortages had spurred communities to find ways to combat starvation, and communal gardens had sprung up everywhere. The coffee shop didn't have coffee, but there was fresh, local fare to be had. He ordered the special, a plate of bacon, eggs and boxty, a delicious potato pancake. As he chewed, his tired gaze drifted to a corkboard on the wall that was peppered with flyers. One handwritten sign advertised fresh eggs from a local farm with a poorly drawn chicken scratching in the dirt.

A flash of memory assailed him: the plump chickens at Keane's farmyard, pecking indiscriminately at the ground. He'd nearly choked on his breakfast as the realization hit him: the biometal kernel may have disappeared, but Bill Masters had nothing to do with it.

He'd taken a risk calling Caitlin from a payphone, but she confirmed that he'd been right to do so and encouraged him to act fast. Stealing the car was the only way to get back to the Keane farm in a hurry. Kevin hated breaking the law, but technically, he was only borrowing the car anyway. He'd be ditching it at the first opportunity.

Whichever one of Keane's chickens had consumed the kernel would be very sick right about now. Kevin was no farmer, but assuming the chicken in question didn't just wander off to die, old man Keane would wonder what had killed a perfectly healthy bird. *Would he take the chicken to the local veterinarian?* Kevin thought not but couldn't be sure. If he did, and if the vet found the kernel and touched it, it would most likely kill him.

Sitting in the stolen car, he shifted back into his own face, but kept the slightly taller, leaner body he'd adopted. He told himself it was because his clothes wouldn't fit otherwise. Tara Keane's fine eyes had no influence on the decision.

He got out of the car and headed for the front door, but it opened before he reached it and Tara slipped out. She was dressed in baggy jeans, combat boots, and a battered green pea coat that was way too big for her. The bandana tied around her head today was pink with yellow happy faces.

She held a finger to her lips and clomped over in the big boots. "Shh," she said when she got close enough. "Me grandfather tied one on again last night and if you wake him, it won't go well for ya. What are you doin' here?"

"I need to see your chickens."

Tara blinked at the bizarre statement and said, "Well, that's a new one."

"I think one of them may have eaten the thing I was looking for yesterday. Remember?"

Her head went back, and she gave him a sharp look. "As if I could forget. How thick do ya think I am? And...are you taller?"

Impatiently, he brushed past her and headed for the chicken coop. "Have any of your chickens gotten sick?"

"No, not sick."

The way she said it, as if there were more to it, made him stop. "What do you mean?"

She shrugged. "The big Sussex hen's always been aggressive, but yesterday she took it to a new level."

Kevin couldn't recall the exact wording Seamus had used in the lore about the Children of the Boar, but he knew the wild boar in the story had acted erratically before it had been slain. An image flashed into his consciousness: that of Astrid, the Swedish scientist on the drill ship who'd died after coming into contact with the biometal. She'd been highly agitated as the ambulance took her away, the whites of her eyes blood red.

44

"Where is it?" he asked.

"The hen? Well...leftovers are in the fridge."

He stared at her, thinking fast. The biometal kernel had made the bird aggressive, so Tara had slaughtered and cooked it for dinner last night before it had even gotten sick. Tara didn't look any worse than she had yesterday; she had the same dark circles under her eyes, but the whites were normal. He rotated his hand in front of his abdomen and asked, "Where are its guts?"

She gave him another strange look but jerked her head towards the pig pen.

He sighed. "You fed it to the pigs?"

"No." She sounded offended. "I buried it in the scrap pile."

He remembered seeing the compost heap and strode off in that direction, Tara trailing behind.

"You said the thing yer lookin' for would kill me if I touched it. The hen wasn't near dead."

"It's not an instantaneous process." He stopped at the approximately two-meter square pile of malodorous mulch, holding a hand to his nose. A chicken-wire cage of sorts had been constructed around the pile, presumably to keep animals out.

Tara flipped the latch and lifted the wooden frame that formed the large hinged lid. Her lips were pressed together, hazel eyes practically twinkling with mirth. "Do ya need the rake, or are you just going to muck about in it?"

He frowned down at his brand-new boots and then bent to roll up the hem of his jeans, loath to get them dirty seeing as how he didn't know when he'd next have access to a washing machine. He stepped over the low fence onto the edge of the mulch pile, grateful when his boot didn't sink very far. His second step produced an ominous squishing sound, but he ignored it. He'd already sensed the biometal, and was now wholly focused on retrieving it. Instead of 'mucking about' in the mulch, he simply bent and held his hand about an inch above the surface, employing the same mental method he'd used to draw it out of the stone. He couldn't see it, but he knew the biometal was working its way through the chicken intestine membrane and the multitude of discarded organic material that made up the pile.

After several minutes, it formed into another kernel right on the surface, where he pinched it between thumb and forefinger and straightened with satisfaction. "Got it."

45

Tara lifted her eyebrows as he tucked it into his coat pocket but didn't comment. She shut the lid and followed him back to the car. "I suppose you'll be leaving again, then?"

Before he could answer, he caught a glimpse of something at the house. Someone, it had to be old man Keane, was watching them from a gap in the curtains. It had been some time since Kevin had gotten that prescient feeling that something was wrong, but it hit hard now. He opened the car door, but it was too late. Through the bare trees lining the long driveway, he saw a dark green sedan, followed by another vehicle, both travelling fast. Their spinning tires sent up clouds of dust from the gravel road, but luckily, they had to slow up some when they began bottoming out on the deep potholes.

Kevin looked at Tara, who sent a hasty glare towards the front window of the house, but she grabbed Kevin's hand and said, "Come on! I know where you can go."

He took a few precious seconds to grab his backpack out of the car and then set off behind her. She tried to run, but the combat boots turned it into more of a shambling trot. As they rounded the side of the house, he thought about abandoning her, but couldn't afford to. She'd grown up here, knew the territory. If anyone could escape their pursuers, it was Tara.

They entered a grove of evergreen trees that provided good cover, but despite Tara's good intentions, she tired quickly. He heard car doors slamming and knew they wouldn't make it at the pace she'd set, even if she could maintain it. She began to wheeze in an alarming manner, breathing in and out rapidly like she was having an asthma attack.

She stumbled on the root of a tree, but he caught her arm before she fell. He looked into her dismayed face and made a split-second decision. He thrust his arms into the straps of his backpack and shrugged it into place. She made a little squeak of protest when he swept her up into his arms, but then she pointed ahead of them down a barely discernible path.

He clutched her frail body to his chest and ran.

Chapter Eleven

Baltimore, Maryland

"So, how do we choose who to waylay?" Lizbeth asked quietly.

They'd abandoned the rental car at the hotel and taken a cab. Each of them had shifted into an anonymous person; Lizbeth was wearing the face of a classmate, and Caitlin had short brown hair and a bland face. They were standing in the airport terminal not far from the United Airline's ticket counter.

Caitlin glanced at the people waiting in line. "I know you haven't practiced with your gossamers much, but you'll find there are those who are easier to establishing mental contact with."

"You mean like someone who's descended from the folk? Can you sense them?" Lizbeth couldn't. She always knew when Caitlin was near because she got a sort of hair-sticking-up-on-the-back-of-her-neck sensation, which would probably be a handy defense mechanism if there were more shapeshifters in the world.

"Not unless they are uncommonly strong, like you, Kevin and Zach were. The vast majority of descendants have very dilute blood, and little or no raw telepathic ability. We can suss them out by process of elimination, though. The average person has weak gossamers, but a descendant's thoughts will seem somewhat louder. Go ahead. If you extend your gossamers and concentrate, you might find a few."

The way she said it suggested she'd already found one. Lizbeth looked at the people in line. Some were talking; some were staring at the ground or off into the distance; others were focused on handheld devices. None of them met her eyes, which meant she couldn't touch their minds. "I can't tell. How do you do it when they won't look at you? And how do you do it while *walking*? It takes so much concentration. I'll never be that good."

"For us, it's quite true the eyes are the window to the soul," Caitlin said. "However, in time, you will find you don't always need to look into their souls to hear them. It takes patience to become an adept."

Lizbeth tried again, shutting her eyes and focusing. After a while, she opened them and said in a dejected tone, "Nothing."

"Don't worry. It will come."

"So why again are we looking for descendants specifically?"

"Reading the average person's mind is generally not a challenge for us; planting a suggestion is another thing altogether. A descendant is more likely to 'hear' us."

Lizbeth recalled the first time she'd met Caitlin. She'd heard her voice in her head clear as day.

Caitlin continued, "Do you see that woman in the red coat near the front of the line?"

Lizbeth didn't make the mistake of staring. Without moving her head, she scanned the area and said, "Yes."

"She's travelling with her sister. They're our marks. Can you read her?"

Lizbeth looked down at her clenched hands, brows scrunched up in concentration, but felt nothing until she shifted her gaze to the woman in the red coat. She gasped. "Yes. I do. She's afraid to fly!"

A proud grin spread over Caitlin's face. "Indeed she is, and we will use that to our advantage, but first, we'll need to segregate them from the crowd and get closer. How do you suppose we should go about it?"

Lizbeth thought about what her grandmother had said. "Plant the suggestion that she needs to pee?"

Caitlin clapped her hands silently. "Good show."

Lizbeth frowned. "I don't understand, though. I didn't think we could make people do things...?"

"We can't. It's not mind control by a long stretch. We simply take advantage of the fact that when a person hears a voice in their head, they will naturally assume it's their subconscious. Especially if we choose our words carefully."

For the next ten minutes, they discussed what words Caitlin would use, and came up with a plan, including several courses of action depending on how their marks, the two sisters who were flying to Dublin, reacted to hearing voices in their heads.

When the women reached the counter to talk with the ticket agent, that was Lizbeth's cue to walk to the nearest women's restroom. Caitlin stayed behind for two reasons: to watch where the women put their tickets and wallets, and to reach out with her gossamers to suggest that the sisters visit the restroom.

Lizbeth went straight to the bathroom counter, set her purse down between two sinks and pretended to fuss over her hair. It was disorienting, as always, to see a face other than her own reflected in the mirror.

A woman in the largest stall was trying to calm a crying child, and a worker with a mop and bucket was waiting outside that stall door. Lizbeth looked into the worker's eyes, offering a commiserating smile as the child's cries escalated. The worker shook her head and made a face, unaware that Lizbeth had made contact with her mind.

Caitlin had given her the task of clearing the restroom, so Lizbeth attempted to insert her voice into the worker's consciousness. She very firmly sent the phrase, "*I'll come back later*," but it didn't appear to have any effect. Caitlin had said dilute descendants of the folk were everywhere, but the worker didn't appear to be one of them.

The stall door opened, and the harried mother came out. The child appeared to be about two years old, and was not only screaming, but twisting and kicking in a violent attempt to escape her mother's arms. The woman glanced at the sink, but apparently decided washing her hands was less important than dealing with her child's full-blown temper tantrum. As soon as she left, the worker began to mop the floor inside the stall.

Lizbeth opened her purse and took out a tube of lip gloss. Just as she'd begun applying it, the woman in the red coat came in, followed by her sister. They looked alike; both were nearing middle age and were of average height and weight, with dark hair and pale, lightly freckled skin. They dragged their luggage into stalls and shut the doors. Caitlin came in and set her satchel on the counter, ignoring Lizbeth. She washed her hands as the worker set out a 'Wet Floor' sign and wheeled her bucket and mop out of the bathroom.

Lizbeth's heart began to beat faster. The smell of bleach from the floor turned her already nervous stomach. She went over the plan again and took several calming breaths. The worst thing that could happen was they wouldn't succeed. The women would have no way of knowing what was going on. None of it felt right to Lizbeth, however. She hadn't even done anything yet but felt guilty. What they were about to do could seriously mess a person up.

One of the stall doors opened and the woman in the red coat came out. Caitlin looked at Lizbeth and sent, "*Wallet, passport and ticket in left coat pocket.*"

The woman pushed up her sleeves and held a hand out to the automatic soap dispenser, but hesitated, staring into the sink. Lizbeth knew that at that moment, Caitlin had spoken in the woman's mind, saying, *"The plane is going to crash."*

Lizbeth snapped the lid onto her lip gloss and dropped it. The tube bounced off the counter and rolled near the woman's feet. Lizbeth bent to retrieve it, bumping gently into the woman and saying, "Oh, sorry."

With years of pickpocketing experience she almost never used illegally, it was easy to lift the wallet and ticket and tuck them into her own pocket. She went back to applying lip gloss, although her mouth was already slick and shiny. Her next target was the woman's sister, who was just leaving the stall, the wheels of her suitcase rumbling on the tile.

Caitlin was pretending to rummage around in her satchel. She sent Lizbeth the information that the sister's wallet, passport and ticket were in a side pocket of the suitcase.

The sister said, "They have a Dunkin Donuts here. You want to stop for coffee?"

The woman opened her mouth, but no words came out. Caitlin was still bombarding her with suggestions that she would die if she got on the plane.

"Vickie?" the sister asked. "You okay?"

Vickie shook her head. There were bright pink splotches on her cheeks. "I think...I think I'm having a panic attack."

"What?" The sister let go of her suitcase handle and grasped Vickie's shoulders, which were rising and falling with her increased breathing.

With a note of hysteria in her voice, Vickie said, "It's like this voice in my head is telling me the plane's going to crash."

Lizbeth squatted down to fuss with the buckle on her boot, unnoticed by the two women. It was easier taking something that wasn't nestled up against someone's body, like the items in Vickie's pocket, but she was also more exposed unzipping the suitcase. If either of the women should happen to hear her or glance down, she'd be caught.

But Caitlin wasn't done. Her focus now turned to the sister. Lizbeth was surprised to actually catch the words Caitlin planted in the woman's mind.

"She's right. The Cataclysm isn't over. The plane is going to crash."

As the woman sucked in a hissing breath, Lizbeth slid the zipper down and reached inside the pocket. She pulled out the plane ticket, passport, and a bulging wallet and left the suitcase unzipped. The wallet was

50

too big for her pocket, so she held it against her thigh as she straightened up, then grabbed her purse and went into one of the stalls. It was easy to find and remove Vickie's driver's license from her wallet, but the sister's wallet was a receipt-and-coupon-filled nightmare. The driver's license was nowhere to be found.

Lizbeth was about to give up when it occurred to her that the sister may have anticipated the need to find it easily and put it in her passport. Sure enough, there it was.

With the tickets, passports and IDs removed, now all she had to do was put the wallets back. Caitlin had been very specific that the sisters would notice their missing *wallets* right away, but might not realize the other items were gone until it was too late.

It was a piece of cake to get the big wallet back into the suitcase and zip it up, but slipping Vickie's back into her pocket was more of a challenge since she and her sister were hugging each other and the pocket in question was facing the mirror.

"It'll be fine," the sister said.

"How do you know? Marcus thought everything would be fine before his plane crashed. He called me from the airport and told me he was going to sleep the whole way!"

Lizbeth winced. It would have been almost impossible to find marks that hadn't lost someone in the Cataclysm, but hearing the agony in Vickie's voice made her want to search out anyone else to waylay.

Caitlin apparently wasn't experiencing the same compunctions. Lizbeth caught the phrase, "*Marcus' spirit is trying to warn you.*" She leaned past the hugging women to give her grandmother a dirty look.

Caitlin merely sent, "*Put the wallet back now.*"

Lizbeth pouted, but did as she was told. Her job was done, so she left and found a bench near the information kiosk where she could keep an eye on the restroom. Every time she felt a pang of regret for what they'd done, and for what Caitlin was continuing to do, she reminded herself that it was her duty as Caitlin's granddaughter to protect what remained of her people from the kind of persecution Bill would bring down upon them. They had to stop him somehow, even if she had to treat people like Vickie and her sister like collateral damage.

Only one other person went into the restroom while Lizbeth sat and waited. That woman had long since come back out by the time the sisters made an appearance. They walked rapidly across the terminal, dragging their luggage. Instead of heading for the concourse to meet their plane, they passed under a sign that read, among other things: *Long-term Parking.*

51

Lizbeth waited while they went through the sliding glass door and marched across the tarmac towards a vast sea of cars before heading back to the restroom. Caitlin was already wearing Vickie's face. Lizbeth disappeared into the stall and came back out looking like Vickie's sister, whose name, according to her driver's license, was Charlotte Doyle.

Caitlin lifted her eyebrows and asked, "Shall we get coffee at Dunkin Donuts?"

Chapter Twelve

San Francisco, California

By the time the inflatable outboard bumped into the side of the ferryboat, Zach had wrapped himself like a fast food burrito in a silver foil emergency blanket. The rescuer who'd performed resuscitation on Seamus had gotten him to breathe on his own, but he hadn't regained consciousness. The man piloting the outboard hooked it up to the same lines that had lowered it and signaled to someone on board the ferry to lift them out of the water.

Zach, normally a quick thinker, was too stunned to come up with a plan. He watched Seamus' chest rise and fall, willing him to come to, but it didn't happen.

Once on board the ferry, crew members transferred Seamus to a portable stretcher. Zach stumbled along behind as they carried the stretcher inside the lower deck. It was warm enough inside that despite still being soaked, his shivering slowly subsided. The captain made an appearance and the rescuer who'd resuscitated Seamus updated him.

The captain took one look at Seamus and asked, "Who the hell is that?"

The rescuer lifted his shoulders slightly and looked to Zach for the answer.

The captain, too, looked pointedly at Zach. "Where's your uncle? I was told he was the one who'd fallen overboard."

Zach couldn't very well deny it when there'd been so many witnesses. "He did. I went in after him, and thought this was him." The explanation was lame at best, but it was the only one that came to mind. Zach would have to act just as confused as everyone else.

"Damn it!" The captain turned to the rescuers. "Well, don't just stand there, get the outboard back in the water and find H.Q. Spencer!"

53

The next hour crawled by as Zach sat miserably waiting in his borrowed wet tuxedo. The coast guard arrived and joined the search. There were no helicopters available to airlift the unconscious one-armed man to the hospital, so he was sent to shore ahead of the ferry in another outboard. Zach was forced to pretend indifference as they took Seamus away; instead he faked concern that his uncle had yet to be found.

When the ferry reached the dock, the police were waiting to interview passengers and crew. Zach and Seamus had planned for this; the officers were from the Marine Unit and had never seen Zach the rookie cop before. Technically, Seamus' plan was still in play, even though it'd taken an unexpected detour. H.Q.'s body would obviously not turn up. Seamus would regain consciousness eventually and most likely claim he'd been a party guest who'd jumped overboard to help rescue the old man. Zach hoped that's how it would pan out anyway.

His hopes were dashed when the first thing the interviewing officer said to him was, "Why did the man you rescued have your uncle's wallet in his pocket?"

Chapter Thirteen

County Wicklow, Ireland

Kevin was in fairly good shape, but if they didn't find a hiding spot soon, he doubted he could keep up the pace he was maintaining long enough to outrun his pursuers – not while carrying Tara. She kept her thin arms twined around his neck except when she needed to point the way.

They left the relative safety of the evergreen trees to cut across a meadow, where the grass was inexplicably green even in the cold weather. On the far side, a grove of huge oak trees grew so close to each other that some of the branches had grafted together, forming a natural barrier.

He spared a glance behind him when they reached the oaks. He heard the occasional shout but didn't see anyone...yet.

Tara struggled out of his arms and slipped between two tree trunks. "This way!"

Beyond the trees, the ground sloped upwards in a low, rocky knoll. Instead of climbing to the top, where they would be exposed, she led him around the knoll, which looked suspiciously like a manmade structure. The weathered sandstone rocks sticking up out of the mossy soil were all about the same size and thickness. Tara went straight for a wide flat rock at the base of the mound.

"Here, help me." She wrapped her fingers around the edge of the unremarkable rock and tried to lift it.

A man's urgent voice echoed on the crisp morning air, "Footprint over here!"

Kevin caught a glimpse of the man; it was the same soldier who'd shot him yesterday when he was a dog. He ducked down before he was spotted and gripped Tara's rock. It was squarish, about the size and thickness of a sewer grate, and heavy. Once they had it balanced at a ninety-

55

degree angle or so, he saw an opening underneath, with stacked rocks forming rough walls on all four sides.

She said, "Hold it steady," and let go of the rock. Then she placed her palms on the edges of the opening and went in feet first. When her combat boots struck bottom, only her head and shoulders were left sticking out. She lifted her arms and grasped the sides of the rock, bracing her backside against the wall and locking her elbows. "Okay, your turn."

A couple of things came to mind: the rock was far too heavy for her, and there wasn't enough room for Kevin next to her, but he bit back his protest. There was no time to argue and the faster he moved, the less time she'd have to spend holding the rock. He let go and quickly took his backpack off and dropped it on the ground. Within seconds he'd slipped into the hole and taken over holding the heavy rock, amazed she'd managed it alone.

She squeezed past him and grabbed his backpack before ducking down and disappearing into the hillside. Kevin bent his knees and lowered the rock more slowly than he'd like, but he didn't want it to slam down and crack into pieces. He pulled his fingers away from the edges at the last second. The entrance to the mound sealed off with a clunk. Unless their pursuers overturned every flat rock on the little hill, they wouldn't find the opening.

There was almost no light; just that little bit that came in around the edges of the stone, but he could see. Ahead of him was a narrow tunnel – but no Tara. He had to turn sideways to navigate the passageway, which turned right abruptly after several meters. After several more meters, the passageway turned left. It was cold, and as the ground sloped slightly downward through what was clearly an ancient cairn, it got colder. It was also pitch black now; even Kevin's enhanced vision couldn't make out the smallest detail. He continued along until the walls that had pressed against him the entire way suddenly opened up.

A light flared from the far side of a large chamber. Tara held up a flashlight and said, "Come on in."

She was sitting cross-legged on a long block of light-colored stone, quartzite if Kevin wasn't mistaken. The stone was the length of a tall man and set against the wall in a curved, recessed alcove. Carved all along the block were swirls just like those on the gossamer crown. Kevin was hardly surprised. This cairn was built on the same land that had produced the biometal the crown was made of. The only surprising thing was that there was no record of the cairn in the maps Kevin had studied.

56

"Welcome to the big family secret," Tara said. "My grandmother's family didn't want any of it to end up in a museum, so we've kept quiet about it over the generations."

He moved farther into the room and sat next to her on the stone. Her boots were resting a few inches from his thighs; she'd pulled her knees up under the pea coat and wrapped her arms around them.

"Are you cold?" he asked.

"Freezin', but that's nothin' new. Not enough meat on me bones for proper insulation."

"How'd they get here so fast?"

"They've set up camp in the village. Told grandfather there was a big reward if you popped 'round again." She paused for a moment before looking down at her knees and adding, "We could use the money. Medical bills, you know."

Medical bills.

Kevin fell silent and looked around the chamber. The rough-hewn rocks that made up the walls were dry and there was no sign that small animals had taken up residence, or for that matter, spiders or other insects. It was as if the room was as untouched as the day it had been built, which, from the method of construction, Kevin estimated to have been some time in the Bronze Age – well before Queen Wyn's time. But he knew places like this were used and built upon by generation after generation over the course of centuries; for all he knew, Wyn herself could be entombed here.

He looked up at the lintels that formed the ceiling, imagining Bill's goons crawling all over the mound looking for them.

"Your grandfather knows about this place," he said.

She nodded slowly. "But I'm fairly sure he doesn't know 'bout the entrance. He married into the family and was never interested in the history of the place. Would've sold the land by now if he could. But it's to go to me. If I live long enough."

"How old are you?" he asked, thinking, *too young to die.*

"Just turned seventeen. You?" She was shivering; he could hear it in her voice.

"Nineteen," he replied, reaching down for his backpack. "I was in college before the Cataclysm."

He propped the backpack against the wall and leaned against it. "Come here."

She hesitated for an instant and then scooted closer. He put his arm around her self-consciously, telling himself the embrace was a strictly platonic sharing of resources: his warmth.

"So what happened after the Cataclysm to make you...whatever it is you are?" she asked.

"Caitlin refers to us as 'the folk' or 'fae.'"

She pulled away enough to look up into his face. "I knew it! You're a fairy."

He frowned and muttered, "Whatever."

She laughed. "It's not a *bad* thing. What can you do besides shapeshift?"

Her hazel eyes looked black in the dim glow from the flashlight. He fought against a rush of tenderness that made him want to kiss her smiling lips. To dispel it, he answered without thinking, "I can read minds."

Her smile faded and she squirmed a little under his arm, murmuring, "Oh," and after a moment, "Well, then."

He said, "I'm not reading you *now*. I don't – I'm not like that."

Her lips curved again. "That's a relief. I wouldn't want ya ta think I'm sweet on ya or anythin'."

The urge to read her mind to confirm what he *thought* she was trying to say was almost overwhelming. He really didn't have a lot of experience around girls. They'd always tended to go for his taller classmates. Even Lizbeth chose tall Zach over him, but suddenly the sting from that rejection didn't hurt anymore. Not with Tara so close smelling like...*lilacs*.

She sighed and laid her head against his chest.

"You okay?" he asked.

"Just tired. Been a while since I did much runnin'."

His arm tightened around her and he rested his chin on top of her head. He hadn't shaved in days, and the dusting of stubble on his jawline rasped against her bandana.

Earlier, when he first realized she'd eaten the tainted chicken, he'd been in too much of a hurry to consider the ramifications, but now it all rushed in. As far as he knew, he and Caitlin were the only ones who'd put two and two together after reading Seamus' stories.

He'd asked her about it.

"If the original three knew, why did they let initiates touch the crown without the protection of the tainted meat?"

She'd given him an answer that reminded him how ruthless his ancestors had been.

"I believe they did know, but the knowledge was either lost or more likely, they kept it to themselves."

"And allowed so many initiates to die?"

"The druids had many enemies who undoubtedly tried to infiltrate their order. Having the ability to pick and choose who joined them would have been invaluable. Besides, what better way to foster fear of the crown? If it was widely known how to properly use it, the druids would have been unable to keep it safe for as long as they did. An object of such great power needs to protect itself."

It was just a theory, though, that a person who ate meat from an animal that had contact with the biometal was afforded protection. Caitlin hadn't known about the lore until after the Cataclysm; hadn't ever had the opportunity to test that theory. Not that she *would*. She'd been dead set against anyone else becoming an initiate – much to Zach's disappointment.

There were so many things Kevin didn't know, and much of what he did know, he didn't understand. But Tara had risked her own safety to help him. She'd kept his secret yesterday and patched him up. Despite her physical limitations, she'd pushed herself to bring him here.

She'd said her doctor told her the latest round of chemo had bought her a whole year, *maybe*. It didn't sound like she had much hope.

The kernel of biometal seemed to be burning a hole in his pocket. People like Kevin – his *kind* – were immune to illness, but what would happen to an initiate who was already ill if they touched the biometal? Even with the theoretical protection of the tainted meat, in Tara's weakened state, contact with the biometal might kill her – and if it didn't, would it *cure* her?

There were too many questions, too many variables. Kevin finally understood Caitlin's reticence to let anyone else take the risk. He looked up at the lintel across from them, staring at three swirls that reminded him of the triskele galaxies and the alien he'd 'spoken' with.

What gave him the right to play God?

Chapter Fourteen

Somewhere over the Atlantic Ocean

Vickie and Charlotte Doyle changed planes at JFK and settled down for the long flight across the pond. Lizbeth, as Charlotte, sat in the window seat trying to read a book she'd picked up at the airport bookstore. She glanced out at the clouds occasionally, worried.

She had a ton of questions for Caitlin but couldn't ask them here on the crowded plane where she might be overheard. First and foremost was the concern that the sisters whose identities they'd stolen would find their documents missing and call the authorities.

The word *"relax"* entered her mind. Startled, she looked into Caitlin's eyes.

"If you need to talk, we can always do it this way," Caitlin sent.

Lizbeth chuckled silently. *"I can't believe I forgot about that."*

"It will become second nature to you soon enough...and don't worry. Even if the sisters do call the police, it's been my experience they won't be taken seriously fast enough to catch us. Especially after the Cataclysm."

It was impossible to put a positive spin on the near destruction of the planet, but acts of terrorism in the states and abroad *had* dwindled. For once, the US wanted no part of the latest war in the Middle East, and for the time being at least, religious extremists were too busy fighting each other in their home territory to plot against the US. Concerns about terrorism hadn't taken a back seat exactly, but resources that would normally have been allocated to prevent it had been directed elsewhere, and vigilance had relaxed.

Caitlin spent the next ten minutes silently lecturing Lizbeth on what to do if they got off the plane and found the police waiting for them. She covered the possible scenarios so thoroughly Lizbeth couldn't help wondering how many she'd personally experienced.

"Most of them," Caitlin responded, reminding Lizbeth yet again that Caitlin had access to her every stray thought. For some perverse reason, the memory of sleeping in Zach's arms came to mind. Lizbeth felt her face go hot, and in an effort to change the direction her transparent thoughts had taken, sent, *"You say there's a scientific explanation for everything we can do, but what about Wolfdogge? How could he track someone just by seeing a picture of them?"*

"I've observed his kind, but never studied them. Felicity believes his breed can bounce an image from mind to mind until it finds one that has seen its target."

"And Caw?" Lizbeth asked. *"Zach thinks Caw can read minds. How is that possible if he's never touched the crown?"*

"The druids conducted all sorts of experiments on animals. Caw and Wolfdogge are an example of what I've been telling you about descendants of the folk."

"Would they be able to shift if they did *touch the crown?"*

Caitlin shook her head no. *"Shifting requires conscious effort. Animals lack the intelligence to accomplish it."*

"But you said the biometal itself is intelligent, right?"

"I said it was alive *in a rudimentary way. It is not intelligent, nor can it impart intelligence to those who encounter it. The closest comparison in our world to the biometal would be a nanobot - something that doesn't yet exist. The Gossamer Sphere was launched with a simple purpose, which the biometal accomplished."*

"That's another thing that's been bugging me. Why send the sphere here? Why change Earth into a communication satellite? I thought our region of space was supposed to be, I don't know, kind of empty."

"That is a question I have no ready answer for, although I've given it much thought. Assuming the creators of the Gossamer Sphere chose Earth and it wasn't an accident that it came here, we can presume there's at least one other intelligent life form in our region of space."

"And they can send messages faster than light. I thought that was supposed to be impossible."

Caitlin made a little "ha" sound. *"Einstein's theory of relativity is still reigning supreme on our planet. It postulates that travel at speeds faster than light is impossible, at least for particles that carry information. But even relativity is only a theory. We've got theories based on theories. I believe the human race is in its infancy when it comes to understanding the makeup of the universe."*

She paused, and Lizbeth got a glimpse into her thought process; Caitlin was thinking how to dumb down the rest of what she wanted to say.

"On our planet," Caitlin sent, *"the way human vision evolved, we see lightning when it strikes, but we perceive the sound of lightning sometime later."*

Lizbeth remembered her mother teaching her how to count after a lightning strike to figure out how far away it was.

"Perhaps in part because of this," Caitlin continued, *"someone long ago deduced that light travels faster than sound. If our ears could hear better, hear the thunder from miles away at the exact moment we saw the lightning, we would experience lightning and thunder together as one event and maybe no one would have even thought to question the speed of sound or light. What I'm trying to say is: we are defined by our senses. Our hearing can detect only certain frequencies and our vision a narrow band of light. We've invented devices that measure sound waves and we've mapped the electromagnetic spectrum. We've enhanced our vision through lenses that see the very small and the very far away. It would seem that our limitations haven't limited us. Unless, of course, you consider that there may be another sense, or senses, that never evolved in us at all, here in this secluded part of space, on this planet. One that even our best scientists cannot imagine."*

"I think I understand what you're saying. Faster-than-light travel is a concept we probably won't understand if they try to explain it because we aren't equipped with the same senses as them."

Caitlin shrugged. *"Either that or they are vastly our superiors in intellect."*

"Do you think they'll be friendly?"

"The creators of the Gossamer Sphere have demonstrated that they aren't overtly hostile, insomuch as they considered our race to be more important than a functioning communication satellite, but now that they are aware of our existence, we can't expect them to ignore us, even if we are the evolutionary equivalent of pond scum."

"That's why you're interested in Arp 247? So we can learn something about them?"

Caitlin rested her head against the seat back. *"I didn't expect to learn much, but it can't hurt to be prepared."*

"Did Sam tell you anything?"

Lizbeth had never been on the receiving end of a slammed door, but Caitlin's abrupt cessation of their telepathic conversation came close. It startled her; that her grandmother would cut her off like that. When Caitlin said curtly, "I'm going to take a nap now," Lizbeth sat in her seat nursing hurt feelings and thinking.

Sam *must* have told Caitlin something, but it was clear she wasn't going to share it with Lizbeth, and that meant only one thing: whatever it was, Caitlin felt Lizbeth needed to be protected from it.

Chapter Fifteen

San Francisco, California

After Zach managed to convince the interviewing officer he had no idea why the one-armed man had H.Q.'s wallet in his pocket, his worry about Seamus turned to anger. It wasn't just that the plan had gone horribly wrong, but Seamus hadn't prepped him properly for such an eventuality. The sheet of paper he'd given Zach to memorize had been heavy with the fictional Dawson Spencer's background information, like where he'd supposedly been born and gone to school, but skimpy on the more current basics. When the officer asked Zach where he lived, he'd been forced to wing it, telling him rather lamely that he was between residences at the moment. Then when the officer asked, "How can we get a hold of you?" Zach had been absolutely stumped.

He'd looked at the officer blankly, mouth open as his sluggish brain refused to produce a plausible answer. Finally, he pulled his cell phone from his damp pocket and said, "Phone's ruined, but I'm staying with my uncle at the Ritz."

Zach assumed that's where Seamus was staying anyway, because he'd told him he always stayed there, but the officer gave him such a long, suspicious look that he had a moment of pure panic. All he could think to do after that was play the part of inconvenienced rich heir. He'd looked down his nose at the officer and blustered, "Look, I'm wet and cold and in shock. I don't see how keeping me here is going to help find my uncle. I'd like to get back to the hotel and make some phone calls. It would be nice if I could let family and friends know what's going on before they see it on the news."

The officer had nodded, but then compounded things by offering to drop him off at the Ritz.

Earlier, Seamus had picked Zach up in a rented Lexus and brought him to the dock. Zach knew where he'd parked the car, but the officer hadn't mentioned finding car keys in the one-armed man's pocket, and he assumed they were probably at the bottom of the bay. A taxi was out of the question, since Zach only had ten bucks on him and there was no way he was going to ask his parents to pay for it once he got home. Just contemplating the questions they would ask made him shudder.

But he couldn't very well stroll into the Ritz. What if the officer came in with him? Zach had no idea if Seamus had been parading around the hotel using his face. Would the hotel staff recognize him and let him into H.Q.'s room? If he had to prove who he was, he'd be in trouble. The driver's license in his pocket didn't exactly have Dawson Spencer's name on it.

In the end, he'd thanked the officer and said he had a ride waiting. It was a simple matter of walking away, followed by the less simple matter of finding and riding a series of buses home. He thought about going to the hospital, but the police would be there, and as Dawson Spencer, he wouldn't have any reason to check up on the one-armed stranger.

After almost four hours availing himself of what passed for bus service in post-Cataclysm San Francisco, he made it home. Caw met him at the front door, and he shook his head at the bird, muttering, "If I was a shapeshifter, I could have flown home, too."

He stripped off his still-damp clothing and looked morosely at his ruined cell phone before remembering something he'd seen on television. Rice was a desiccant; it should dry out the circuits of his phone – if it wasn't already too late. He removed the battery and SIM card before padding barefoot into the kitchen and stuffing the phone down in the storage container of rice his mother kept in the pantry.

He then stumbled to the bathroom for a hot shower before falling into bed and passing out, secure in the knowledge that Seamus would escape from the hospital as soon as he regained consciousness.

When the alarm went off two hours later, he started to get up, but realized it was Saturday and gratefully lay back down. As he was dozing off, he wondered how Seamus had lost his arm. *The guild probably clapped him in irons and he chewed it off,* he thought.

After a moment, his eyes opened and he looked up at the cracks in the ceiling. The police would have Seamus handcuffed to the rail of his hospital bed. Zach was a police recruit and he knew a little something about handcuffs – they were made of steel, and steel was mostly iron.

Seamus can't shift while he's in handcuffs.

Despite his exhaustion, Zach jumped out of bed, got dressed and grabbed his backpack. He stuffed an extra pair of jeans, a shirt, socks and shoes inside. He thought about taking his gun but decided against it.

He didn't know how he would do it, but he was going to have to rescue Seamus.

Chapter Sixteen

County Wicklow, Ireland

Kevin opened his eyes to darkness and lifted his head. His neck was stiff and sore. It took a moment to connect his discomfort with his location, and when he realized he'd fallen asleep sitting up in the cairn, he called out, "Tara?"

"I'm here." With a little *click*, the flashlight came on. He squinted as the brightness spotlighted his face briefly before she directed the beam elsewhere.

She was sitting across from him with her back against the far wall. *Why had she left him alone on the long stone to sit over there in the cold?*

"What's wrong?" he asked.

"Um...well," she replied slowly, "you were talkin' in your sleep."

"I was?" He was surprised; he'd never done it before – that he was aware of anyway.

"Yeah. And you weren't speakin' English."

"What was I speaking?"

Tara struggled to a standing position and crossed her arms. "I've no idea. It wasn't anythin' I recognized."

Kevin tried to remember what he'd been dreaming, but only came up with the vague image of the triskele galaxies that had been burned into his mind months ago. "I speak several languages. Sorry if it weirded you out."

She lifted a hand to her mouth and bit down on the thumbnail, watching him with an almost wary intentness. "They've probably given up on findin' us by now. What are you goin' ta do?"

Caitlin wouldn't arrive until sometime the next morning. Before Tara's grandfather had called the goon squad on him, Kevin had been planning to spend the afternoon scoping out the Dublin Zoo where Caitlin had asked him to meet her, but he wasn't about to tell Tara that.

"I don't know," he said.

"You never did answer me before, about what happened to change you."

There was a faintly plaintive note, almost a longing in her voice. It reminded him of Bill's desperation when he told Caitlin, "Now I'm either going to join you or die."

Kevin stretched his legs, thinking. He couldn't tell Tara the full truth, but she deserved an answer that would at least satisfy her curiosity. "The Cataclysm wasn't 'chaotic coincidence' like the scientists would like us all to believe."

She took a step closer, avidly interested now. "What was it?"

He took a deep breath and released it in a heavy sigh, already regretting the impulse to tell her. "The truth is even harder to believe."

She snorted impatiently. "What's harder to believe than fairies?"

She had him there. He shrugged and responded, "That the earth is a big communication satellite for aliens?"

Even in the dim light he saw her eyes go wide. After a moment, she said, "Yes. Yes, that would be a bit much to swallow. I take it it's true?"

He stood and slung his backpack over one shoulder. "Pretty much."

She shook her head at him. "And that's it? That's all you're goin' to tell me? Because I had some time to think while you were sleepin' and I came to my own conclusions about a few things."

"Yeah, what's that?"

Her gaze dropped and she appeared to be studying his boots. "I think you lied to me about what was in our mine."

That got his attention. "Why do you say that?"

"Pieced it together. Mr. Masters told us there was unexploded ordnance in there, but he also said it was a matter of national security."

"Okay."

"He wants what you took – badly. And whatever it is, it's not dangerous for *you* to touch." Her chin lifted and she said defiantly, "I think it's what changed you, and that's why you want to keep it out of their hands."

Kevin blinked, stunned. He'd brought this on himself. He could have prevented it by not telling her the truth; not shifting in front of her that first time and confirming what he was. Caitlin was always hammering home how dangerous trusting non-folk was, but he'd been careless. He'd revealed just

68

enough that Tara had figured everything out on her own. Now his instinct was to deny, deny, deny.

He opened his mouth to refute it, but she reached into the pocket of her pea coat and withdrew something. He knew what it was before he saw the kernel resting in the center of her palm, but his hand automatically slid into his own pocket to confirm it was no longer there.

After a long moment in which he could only stare at her in disbelief, she asked, "Am I going to die, then?"

He subsided back down on the long stone and let his backpack fall from his shoulder. "Maybe."

"Oh, so now it's 'maybe'?"

She sounded angry, and he narrowed his eyes at her in response. "Yes. Most people who come into contact with the biometal die. Not all, but most. Why do you think Masters was wearing a Hazmat suit yesterday?"

Her defiance didn't fade. "What happens to the ones who don't die?"

He extended his hand and after a small hesitation, she gave him the kernel. He tucked it back into his pocket, moved his backpack, and ordered, "Sit."

She planted herself next to him, spine ramrod straight. He took the flashlight from her and shone it into her eyes. She flinched away from the light as if it hurt, but not before he took note of the pinkness in the whites. Not red, like Astrid's, although he'd been told his own eyes had been bright red, too, and he'd survived. Heck, Lizbeth hadn't shown any signs of sickness at all, and she'd been the first of them to change. The eye thing wasn't an accurate indication of survival, then.

"How do you feel?" he asked.

Her shoulders slumped a little. "Tired, to be honest, but that's nothin' new. How long does it take? To find out one way or the other, I mean."

Caitlin might know, but Kevin didn't have a clue. "I think it's different for everyone."

"You think? Don't ya know?"

He grimaced. "I'm new at this, okay? All I know is that descendants of the – if you have an ancestor who was like me, you have a better chance of surviving." No way was he going to mention the tainted meat. When she got back to her house, the men who'd chased them would certainly question her, probably under duress.

Then it occurred to him: he couldn't *let* her go back home, and not just for her own safety. Assuming she survived, there was a chance Bill would find out what she'd become. Then the government would have their hands on a star lab rat. It was too big of a risk.

He stood and swung his backpack over his shoulders. "You asked me before to take you with me. Now you don't have a choice. Let's go."

She jumped up, a wide grin on her face. "Lead on, Macduff."

Chapter Seventeen

Dublin, Ireland

When the seatbelt light went out, Lizbeth unclipped hers and stretched her stiff legs, yawning widely. Bustling sounds and murmuring rose from the passengers as the plane taxied to the terminal. Caitlin reached under the seat in front of her and pulled her satchel into her lap. Lizbeth followed suit with her bulging purse.

"What time is it?" she asked.

Caitlin took her prepaid cell phone out of the satchel's side pocket and glanced at the display. "Five a.m. Dublin time."

"What is it our time?"

"Midnight."

"Ah. That's why I feel like creamed death on toast." Lizbeth hadn't napped nearly as long or as often as Caitlin had during the flight.

It seemed to take forever for the line of passengers to grab their luggage from the overhead bins and file out of the plane. The temperature dropped significantly when she stepped into the jet bridge tunnel. She glanced out the window of a narrow door to her left and saw a green tractor pulling an empty train of linked luggage carts.

Once they'd exited the tunnel and she was walking on solid ground again, Lizbeth sighed in relief. The terminal was filled with people, and she stayed close behind Caitlin as they maneuvered their way through the crowd. Then Caitlin stopped and turned so suddenly Lizbeth almost ran into her.

"*Wait,*" Caitlin sent.

Talking mind-to-mind wasn't the same as verbal communication; inflection was muted, emotion difficult to detect. Caitlin's expression gave nothing away. Even so, Lizbeth knew she was communicating a warning.

She met Caitlin's eyes. "*What's wrong?*"

71

"I've been scanning the crowd since we stepped off the plane. There are four men strategically positioned around us. All are completely blank. Their gossamers are invisible to me. They're wearing identical hats – which I suspect are lined with something that is blocking me."

Lizbeth knew better than to look around. *"Iron?"*

Caitlin inclined her head slightly and Lizbeth caught a flash of what had to be one of Caitlin's old memories; that of an angry-looking bearded man wearing full armor. *"It's an old Guild trick,"* Caitlin sent. *"This is bad."*

"But they don't know we know, right?"

"If it's Guild, they know. If it's the British government, maybe not. Either way, we need to get out of here."

Warily, Lizbeth lifted the long strap of her purse over her head so it crossed her chest, and adjusted the bag so it sat at the small of her back. *"Should we shift into new faces?"*

Caitlin scanned the crowd casually. Out loud, she said, "It's too late. They're closing in. You remember what I told you?"

Caitlin had *told* her they would be okay; that even if the sisters contacted the authorities, she and Caitlin wouldn't be caught. But now wasn't the time for recrimination. In this scenario, Caitlin had told her they should split up. She would distract the men while Lizbeth got away.

"I don't want to leave you," Lizbeth sent.

"There's no time. Do as you're told. If they catch us both, we will disappear."

Caitlin stepped away from her, and, probably to cause a commotion that would bring attention to herself, shoved the person in front of her. Then she began to run, clumsily bumping into people; making herself look simple to catch.

Lizbeth hesitated only long enough to identify the men – easy to spot because they immediately began pursuing Caitlin – all but one. Three black baseball caps went after Caitlin, but the third turned towards Lizbeth. He wasn't far away, maybe ten yards or so, but a whole bank of occupied seats was between them. She met his eyes briefly. He took one step in her direction and she bolted. Rather than plow through the crowd like Caitlin had, she ran the opposite way, back into the now empty jet bridge tunnel.

The sound of her boot heels striking the thinly carpeted floor echoed like thunder. Near the end of the tunnel, an airline steward was pushing an old woman in a wheelchair. Both looked at Lizbeth with their mouths open as she flew past.

72

She heard the agent enter the tunnel, but she'd reached her destination: the door at the end. Luck was with her: the handle turned. If it had been locked, she'd have been trapped. As she slipped through onto a metal platform at the top of a set of stairs, the steward shouted, "Hey! You can't go out there!"

She took the steps two at a time, her purse bouncing against her back. By the time she reached the tarmac, she had a tentative plan and a new face – a strikingly beautiful, well-known face.

She expected the agent to be right on her heels but heard muffled shouting and realized the steward must have prevented him from following her. It was a reprieve of sorts, but as soon as the agent identified himself, he'd be after her again.

She headed straight for two airline employees near the plane's open baggage hold. One was sitting at the wheel of the green tractor she'd seen earlier. The other, a young man with badly pockmarked skin, stood staring as she ran up.

"You're – you're..." he spoke in a near-whisper, face the picture of shocked adoration.

"Yes! I am." She mimicked the throaty tones of the famous actress she'd shifted into. "And I need your help. The paparazzi are chasing me. How fast can that thing go?" She gestured to the tractor.

The older man at the wheel stood up halfway out of his seat and leaned over to offer her his hand. "If we get a head start, we can outrun the gits. Let's do a legger!"

She let him hoist her up into the passenger seat, while the other man unhooked the carts and then jumped onto the shelf behind the seats. The driver shifted into gear and started across the tarmac just as a man shouted, "Stop!"

She didn't look behind her; didn't want the agent to see her face and confirm she was a shapeshifter, not to mention figure out how she'd gotten the airline employees to abandon their work to help her.

The tractor was not fast. It was an electric vehicle designed for pulling, not racing. They were travelling at maybe twenty-five miles per hour, making their way around an airplane identical to the one she'd arrived in. The cold air was thick with fuel exhaust.

Despite her intention of hiding her face from the agent, Lizbeth glanced back just long enough to see him standing on the metal platform. He hadn't even come down the stairs, and it looked like he was talking on his cell phone. Just as it occurred to her that he hadn't come after them because he'd called the cavalry, the driver said, "We've got company."

73

Ahead of them, a dark green sedan accompanied by an airport emergency vehicle was speeding to cut them off. Lizbeth's heart sank as the tractor driver stopped and offered her a gap-toothed smile. "Look who's here. Security will see to it you're left alone by those vultures."

There was nothing she could do but smile back and say, "Thank you."

The young man tapped her respectfully on the shoulder and then shoved a piece of paper and a pen under her nose. "Might I have an autograph, Miss?"

She scrawled the actress' name on a grease-stained invoice of some kind, all the while aware that three men had exited the green sedan and were closing in. She fleetingly considered trying to shift into a bird or something but knew she wouldn't even be able to strip off her clothes before they caught her. Even if she managed to launch herself into the air and figure out how to fly, there was no guarantee they wouldn't shoot her down.

She jumped out of the tractor and walked towards them. Two of the men were strangers, but the third was Bill Masters. "Don't run," he said, his voice conveying an unnecessary warning. All three men wore black baseball caps and one had his hand inside the front of his jacket. She didn't see a weapon, but the threat was there.

The baggage handlers waved as the tractor made a slow U-turn and headed back the way it came. One of the men with Bill crossed his arms and smiled. He had dark skin with clusters of even darker freckles next to his wide nose. Something in his manner told her his authority was equal to or greater than Bill's. The radio clipped to his belt was broadcasting the voices of at least two men: "Damn it, where is she?" "The ventilation system!" "That's impossible, it's too small."

Lizbeth relaxed ever-so-slightly. They hadn't caught Caitlin...yet. Her grandmother's words came back to her: *If they catch us both, we will disappear.*

"Who are you?" Bill asked.

Lizbeth had a moment of sudden clarity; a solution so bold she doubted her ability to carry it out – but she had to try.

Without a word, she shifted. A look of fascinated revulsion crossed the freckled man's face and the other man tugged on the brim of his hat as if to ensure it was securely situated on his head. Bill didn't react.

A slight breeze blew a strand of long, curly red hair across her face. "Hello, William," she said, in a passable imitation of her grandmother's voice.

"Caitlin."

74

She gestured to his radio. "Call off the chase. Let Lizbeth go and I'll cooperate fully."

Chapter Eighteen

San Francisco, California

Zach did something he'd never done before and would very likely never get the chance to do again: borrowed his parents' car without asking. Theirs was a traditional Chinese American household and respect for your elders was not just expected, it was enforced. Zach's dad was actually his stepfather, who'd raised him from a young age. Zach loved him, although he occasionally wished his mother had found someone a little more easy-going. His dad was not only strict, but quick to anger – and that anger was slow to fade. He was prone to delivering long lectures that bordered on emotional abuse.

Zach had been forced to sit through many of those lectures, struggling to rein his own anger in. In one of his rare introspective moments, he'd decided his tendency to poke fun at everything was a stopgap for that anger. Cracking jokes in the face of a tongue lashing might fuel his dad's anger, but Zach's only other options were to run from it or fight back. For someone as well trained in the martial arts as he was, fighting back was not an option.

When his dad found the apologetic sticky note Zach left in the middle of the kitchen table, he was going to be furious and there was nothing Zach could do about it. He scooped up the car keys from the porcelain bowl on the sideboard and went into the garage. Before he got into his parents' Explorer, he took his dad's folding bolt cutters out of the tool chest and stuffed them into his backpack.

As he drove, he concocted a half-baked plan to schmooze his way into Seamus' hospital room and cut the handcuffs off. Seamus could then change into the clothes he'd brought, shift into another face and walk out. Zach would wait a few minutes and walk out, too. He didn't have a plan for what would happen if the officer guarding Seamus' room got suspicious and detained him.

In the likely event they'd need to make a quick getaway, he drove around the hospital parking lot until he found a relatively close spot. Inside the hospital, he waited in line at the main information desk. When he reached the front, he put his elbows on the counter and leaned towards the heavy-set receptionist, whose thick eyebrows were separated only by deep frown furrows.

"Hi there," he said with as much charm as he could muster. "San Francisco PD brought in a suspect last night. What room's he in?"

"And you are...?"

Zach said the first thing that popped into his head. "His brother."

"Third floor." She looked past him to the next person in line and he slid away sideways, not willing to argue the fact that she hadn't given him the room number. Probably he'd see the guard outside the door and figure it out on his own.

But the third floor had no guard. In fact, there was no obvious police presence at all, just hospital employees and a few visitors here and there. Zach walked down the main corridor, glancing down side hallways and avoiding the nurses. He peeked into as many rooms as he could but didn't see Seamus. With no other recourse, he finally approached a nurse's station and waited for one of the two women working there to notice him. The one wearing pink scrubs glanced up and asked, "Can I help you?"

"Yes, thank you. Um, last night the police brought in a suspect and they told me downstairs he was on this floor."

"Right. Are you next of kin?"

Zach frowned, concerned now. "Yeah."

She stood and reached for a file in a sorter. "I wasn't on shift when he came in, but I do know they've moved him to ICU for the time being."

"ICU? Did he regain consciousness?"

"No. Dr. Freeman is the attending physician and can fill you in on what's going on, Mr...?"

"Smith." It came out before he realized how lame of an alias it was, but the nurse simply said, "And your brother's name? The police didn't know who he was."

"Roger. Roger Smith."

"Okay. I'm going to need you to fill out some paperwork. Have a seat while I page Dr. Freeman."

Zach nodded and let his backpack slip off his shoulder. The bolt cutters made an overly loud clunk when the backpack hit the floor, but the nurse didn't seem to notice. He subsided into one of two side chairs with stained floral upholstery and took the clipboard she handed him. He dutifully filled out the paperwork, making everything up on the fly and using barely legible handwriting. That took only ten minutes of the thirty he sat there trying not to look guilty. If only he'd taken the time to check to see if his phone had dried out. A soothing game of Finger Fiddle would settle his nerves.

"Mr. Smith?"

Zach's head jerked up. He'd actually dozed off sitting in the uncomfortable chair. He lurched to his feet and mumbled, "Yeah, that's me."

"I'm Dr. Freeman."

Zach shook the doctor's hand. He was a white guy, just past middle age if the grey at his temples was any indication, and had perfect teeth. He looked to Zach like one of those infomercial actors who say, "I'm not a real doctor, I just play one on TV."

"I'm afraid your brother Roger was gravely injured last night," Dr. Freeman said. "Did the police explain the circumstances?"

"Uh, yeah. Drowning and – and hypothermia?"

Dr. Freeman nodded. "His pupils were nonreactive, so we did an MRI, which looked normal, but the EEG, I'm sorry to say, showed no brain activity whatsoever."

Zach opened his mouth, but for once, no words came out.

Dr. Freeman put a hand on his shoulder. "I'm sorry."

Zach could only stutter, "He's – he's *brain dead*?"

Dr. Freeman sighed, a conflicted sound. "He's breathing on his own, which is a good sign, but...well...we'll do another EEG in twenty-four hours to confirm. Does your brother have a living will and do you know if he's an organ donor?"

Zach ignored the fact that Dr. Freeman's questions, so soon after notifying Zach that his 'brother' might be essentially dead, weren't exactly tactful. All he could think was, *no wonder there wasn't a guard outside his door.*

After a short hesitation, he replied shakily, "I don't know. Can I see him?"

Dr. Freeman blinked a few times, tilted his head and said, "You're Asian, but your brother looked Caucasian."

Zach had regained his composure. "He's my older half-brother. Our dad's white. Can I see him?"

He halfway expected to be asked to show his ID, but the doctor must have assumed since Zach got this far, he was who he said he was.

"This way." Dr. Freeman walked down the main hallway and took a right. There was another nurse's station, occupied by a man in blue scrubs who stood when he saw them. Dr. Freeman ignored him.

The room had two beds, but only one was being used. Seamus lay on his back, face pale, black hair loose on the pillow. An intravenous line trailed away from his arm and a cardiac monitor beeped rhythmically. The stump of the other arm wasn't visible, but from the shape under the hospital gown Seamus was wearing, had been severed high on the arm below the shoulder.

Dr. Freeman examined one side of the bed and then walked around to look at the other. He turned to the nurse. "Where's his catheter?"

The nurse looked confused. "What do you mean?"

Dr. Freeman gestured towards Seamus. With obvious contempt, he said, "This man has no catheter and – damn it, there's a kink in his line! Is it too much to ask that you do your *job*?"

"I just got on shift," the nurse protested weakly.

Zach edged past the doctor and leaned over to look into Seamus' face. He nearly jumped out of his skin when Seamus' eyes opened. The doctor was still berating the male nurse as Zach leaned closer and whispered, "Seamus?"

"Took you long enough," Seamus whispered back with a smile and a wink. He jerked his head towards the doctor and closed his eyes again.

Zach straightened up and turned to Dr. Freeman, raising his voice to get his attention. "May I please have a few moments alone with my brother?"

Dr. Freeman stopped mid-sentence and pressed his lips together. "Certainly."

As he and the nurse disappeared down the hallway, Zach heard him start in again, "It's a miracle he hasn't wet the bed...except, of course, he wasn't getting any *fluids...*"

As soon as they were out of range, Zach pulled the curtain to hide Seamus, who sat up, removed the IV from his arm and said, "Did you bring clothing?"

"Yeah." Zach hurriedly unzipped his backpack and pulled everything out. "What happened?"

Seamus shrugged. "Must have hit the water wrong and knocked myself out."

He stripped off his gown and pointed to the cardiac monitor. "See that orange button that says 'Silence Alarms'? Press it."

Zach did as he was told and winced for Seamus as he ripped the sticky electrode pads from his chest. When Seamus slid out of bed to put on the jeans, Zach turned and peeked around the curtain to keep an eye out and give him some privacy.

From behind him, Seamus chuckled and said, "The bolt cutters are a nice touch."

"I figured the police would have you cuffed to your bed."

"They would have, but for a few tricks I learned some years ago."

Zach had an 'aha' moment. "You kept your pupils from reacting to the light. But how did you turn your brain waves off?"

"It takes a lot of practice and discipline, but I can control my gossamers long enough to fool their machines."

"That's brilliant. No need to cuff the brain dead," Zach said. "How'd you keep the nurse from giving you a catheter? Mind control?"

"No, that was sheer blind luck, but I did kink the fluid line. No point blowing the whole thing because I couldn't hold my bladder until you got here."

A few seconds later, Seamus was dressed and wearing a different face. He'd also sprouted a new arm. "You have a car?"

"Burgundy Explorer on the south side of the main parking lot, third aisle down," Zach said.

Seamus nodded, poked his head out from behind the curtain, looked both ways, and walked off.

Zach put his backpack on and counted slowly to ten before striding confidently away – perfect timing, as it turned out, since Dr. Freeman was on his way back.

"Mr. Smith," the doctor said. "I want to apologize for what you heard. I'll be placing an incident report in Nurse Messina's file. I assure you the care your brother is receiving here is our utmost priority."

"Thank you, doctor. If you'll excuse me, I have...arrangements to make."

Dr. Freeman seemed slightly taken aback, but he said, "Of course. Again, let me say how sorry I am for your loss, and please – I know you must be in shock, but keep in mind your brother's organs could save lives."

Zach nodded and ducked his head as if he were overwhelmed with grief. The elevator was only a few yards away, and someone, not Seamus, was just getting on. He tossed the doctor a tight smile and broke into a jog to catch it. Thankfully, it went straight to the lobby with no stops. He knew he didn't have much time before Dr. Freeman or a nurse realized Seamus was gone.

Chapter Nineteen

Dublin, Ireland

The Dublin Zoo reminded Kevin of the zoo in San Antonio, the only other one he'd ever visited. He didn't know if it was the mildly unpleasant smells from the animal enclosures or the screeching and calling of the exotic birds and monkeys, but as he and Tara strolled along the pathways, a sense of déjà vu nagged at him.

They'd walked a meandering course for the Snow Leopard exhibit, where Caitlin was supposed to meet them, but after lingering outside the enclosure for nearly an hour, he decided they'd best move on. It wasn't as if the one leopard in view was providing them with scintillating entertainment; the animal had been sleeping with its back to them the whole time. They wandered away to look at the orangutans, wolves and tigers before stopping at an outdoor café for a late breakfast.

Tara wore a jaunty red knit cap over a shoulder-length blonde wig. She kept sticking her finger under the edge of the cap and scratching, and when Kevin pointed it out to her, she said, "It itches something fierce!"

The itching seemed to be her only complaint. The whites of her eyes were normal. Not only had she shown no sign of illness over the last twelve hours, but she'd perked up significantly after her initial weakness in the cairn. They'd left the cairn under cover of the Cataclysm's unnaturally darkened skies, which produced long and early twilights. After several miles hiking through neighboring farmers' fields, they encountered a lonely road. They'd followed the road for an hour or so, Tara keeping up with the brisk pace he set without protest.

The driver of a wooden-sided lorry piled high with battered household appliances that seemed destined for the dump pulled over and offered them a ride. Kevin warily accepted, worried that the driver wasn't who he seemed, but the man had dropped them outside of Dublin without incident. Turned out they weren't far from the hostel where Kevin had stayed the night before, and they managed to get two beds. In the morning, they'd taken a bus to another department store, where he purchased Tara shoes that fit, a decent coat, two outfits, a backpack, some girly supplies, and the itchy wig.

Another bus had delivered them to the zoo.

At the café, Tara ordered a hearty breakfast of sausage, eggs and potatoes, which she proceeded to chow down before Kevin had hardly begun eating his scone. She swigged the last of her sweet tea and looked casually around at the other patrons before asking quietly, "How long are we goin' ta wait for them?"

"As long it takes."

"What if we wait all day and they don't show?"

"They will." Kevin was more concerned about whether Caitlin would be able to identify him. She was looking for only one person, and she'd never seen the face he wore now; that of a scruffy blonde surfer type.

"What if they don't?" Tara persisted.

"Then we'll figure something out."

"Is there...a place you all go?"

Kevin had been observing the people around them, reaching out to see if he could sense them. Any two people together got a second look but were quickly eliminated as not being petite enough to be Caitlin and Lizbeth. Tara's words took a moment to register, but when they did, he responded with a scoffing laugh. "You mean like vampires hanging out at the local castle? You watch too much TV."

"I prefer to read, thank you very much, and I didn't think the question was unreasonable considerin' you've told me bugger all."

He didn't turn his head, just shifted his eyes to direct a mildly scornful gaze her way. Words of censure were on the tip of his tongue, but he didn't utter them. Her normally pale cheeks were pink from the cold, and the dark circles under her eyes had vanished. He'd been waiting for the right moment to test her, and this appeared to be as good a time as any.

"*How do you feel?*" he sent.

"Fine," she replied. It must have been an automatic response, because as soon as she said it, she frowned and stared at his mouth. "Did you...?"

"*Speak? No.*"

"Oh. Right. The mind reading thing."

"*Try it,*" he sent.

"What?" A hint of something appeared in her eyes, hope mixed with doubt.

He smiled. *"Say something without moving your lips."*

She must have sensed sarcasm, because she twisted those lips and sent, *"Like what? That you're a cheeky git?"*

Kevin snorted and said out loud, "If you say so."

She stared at him. "You heard me? What does it mean?"

"'Cheeky git'? I don't know exactly, but I don't think it was a compliment."

She snatched the nearest thing that came to hand – a packet of jelly – and threw it at him. "You know what I mean!"

He lifted a shoulder. "Not sure, but only the folk can talk to each other that way."

To his surprise, she shoved her chair back and stood. "I'll be right back."

"Where are you going?"

"The loo."

He watched her back as she stalked away, synthetic blonde hair bouncing with every step. Her new jeans weren't fancy – at the department store, she'd headed straight for a rack of plain and serviceable Levi's, but they fit well, despite her narrow hips. The black coat and blue and white tennis shoes, too, were utilitarian. The hat was the only thing about her that stood out, that and the fake blonde hair.

She was gone for twenty minutes; longer than he liked. When she returned, he was all geared up to lecture her on how important it was that they stick together, but as she sat in her chair, the expression on her face stopped him. He'd seen her smile before, seen the way it lit her up from the inside, but this smile more than glowed – it captured and reflected nothing less than every secret in the universe. Her bright blue eyes watched him closely, like she was gauging his reaction...*to what?*

Then it hit him. Tara's eyes were hazel, not blue – and the hair peeking out from under the red cap was no longer a fake, brassy blonde. She must have seen his dawning comprehension, because she pulled the cap off and shook her head, freeing soft, cascading waves of *real* hair with a delighted laugh. "Look at me!"

He wouldn't have prevented his answering smile if he could. "You look beautiful."

She jumped out of her chair and came around the table, grinning widely. He thought she was going to hug him, but instead, she put her cold hands to his face and swooped in for a kiss.

84

It was hard and quick, a peck really, but Kevin felt the heat rise in his cheeks. She kept hold of his face and looked into his eyes, her own brimming with unshed tears.

"I've never been so happy in all my life. Thank you doesn't cover it."

She kissed him again, with soft lips that lingered this time. Her mouth tasted like sausage, but not in a bad way.

Kevin was torn. Her gratitude was entirely misplaced; he was only peripherally responsible for the change in her. He knew the right thing would be to gently extricate himself from the situation, but he couldn't make himself do it – and not just because it had been a long time since a girl had paid this kind of attention to him. He genuinely liked Tara and had to actively fight the urge to pull her closer.

A voice came from somewhere over her shoulder took the decision out of his hands.

"Excuse me."

Even before Tara pulled away and turned, he knew it was Caitlin. He swallowed nervously, gearing himself up to explain all that was Tara, but Caitlin didn't give him a chance to say a word. She wore dirty, paint-spattered green coveralls and had a nondescript older woman's face.

Her brown eyes cold and hard as permafrost, she sent, *"Lizbeth has been taken."*

Chapter Twenty

Somewhere over the Irish Sea

Bill stayed by Lizbeth's side the entire trip to 'The Facility.' No one spoke to her directly, but that's what they kept calling it, The Facility, like it was too top-secret to have a real name.

She wasn't restrained or blindfolded, but they did take her purse. Then they tucked her into the green sedan and drove towards the ocean, to a flat, remote stretch of land. On the right side of the road were several identical domed metal structures streaked with rust, and on the left side was row after row of what used to be airplanes. She couldn't help but think of all the airplanes that had gone down during the Cataclysm, but these planes were intact, while most of the ones that had fallen from the sky when the earth's magnetic field reversed had been completely destroyed.

At the end of the road was a wide dirt lane, and at the end of that lane was a helicopter, which was apparently their destination.

Lizbeth had never been on a helicopter before and wasn't looking forward to it. The one waiting for them was painted black with grey and white stripes but had no identifying logo. Inside, it seated six; one seat next to the pilot's chair and two sets of bucket seats facing each other in the main cabin. The agent in charge, the dark-skinned freckled man whose name she hadn't caught, sat next to the pilot. Bill took the seat next to her and the third agent sat across from him. That agent was named Collins, and he wore wire-rimmed glasses that made him look more like a middle-grade schoolteacher than a trained MI6 agent. From his permanent glower and the furtive glances he kept sneaking her way, it was apparent he was glad to be seated as far away from her as possible.

Takeoff was loud and disorienting, and did nothing to ease the cold sense of fear she'd been experiencing since the moment they'd caught her.

Bill's presence didn't help matters. He was just as handsome as she remembered, and so overly solicitous of her she was uncomfortable to the point of being creeped out. Of course, he thought she was Caitlin, so it was only natural for him to touch her every chance he got and for his gaze to linger on her face lovingly. In fact, his gaze wasn't just lingering, he was flat-out staring. Once they'd gotten underway, she kept her head averted to look out the window at the ocean below. She could still see his face reflected in the glass, however, and his expression seemed to alternate between longing and regret.

She wanted to yell at him, tell him what a jerk he was for betraying Caitlin and the rest of them. Blinking back tears, she stared out at the hazy horizon and tried not to think about what they had in store for her.

It wasn't a long flight, maybe an hour. From above, The Facility looked like a long, one story warehouse squatting in a gully denuded of vegetation. It was hard to tell distances, but Lizbeth thought the building was isolated from its closest neighbors by several miles at least. The pilot headed for a large white circle painted on the eastern end of the roof. As they began their descent, Bill took Lizbeth's hand. She snatched it away and refused to look at him, thinking, *Does he really think Caitlin would forgive him so easily?*

To her surprise, Bill's fingers closed around her wrist. She glared at him but said nothing. If only she could read his mind, or better yet, like the real Caitlin, put a choice phrase or two into his head. She'd tell him in no uncertain terms what she thought of him. Not that the stupid hat on his head would let her.

He was still staring intently at her, like *he* was attempting to read *her* mind. She tried to pull her arm away, but he only tightened his grip. Despite the hat, she was so angry she put everything she had into sending the word, "*Jerk.*"

The last thing she expected was to get a response.

"*I'm here to help you.*"

She froze, and after a heartbeat or two sent, "*You can hear me?*"

He leaned closer, maintaining eye contact. When he repeated the phrase, "*I'm here to help you,*" she realized that of course he couldn't hear her. All the staring was simply to tell her through body language that she should try to read him.

He would just keep repeating himself until she acknowledged him, so she nodded, looking up at his baseball cap. It looked just like the ones worn by the pilot and the agents, but Bill must have altered it – removed whatever they'd lined it with.

87

His grip on her wrist relaxed and he let out a sigh. He glanced at Agent Collins, but the other man was reading something on his phone.

Bill looked back into her eyes, obviously inviting her to read him again, so she did.

"I never meant for it to get this far. I'm so sorry."

Chapter Twenty-one

San Francisco, California

Zach pulled into the empty parking space next to Seamus' rented Lexus and asked, "What now?"

Seamus shifted into H.Q. Spencer and replied, "A very confused old man is about to come back from the dead."

"What? Why would you do that?" Zach didn't want everything he'd been through in the last twenty-four hours to be for nothing – especially since he was supposed to have gotten a ton of money out of the deal.

"I heard the cops talking in the hospital," Seamus said. "It's amazing what people will say in front of you when they think you're comatose. They suspect this wasn't an accident, and they think my nephew was involved. I'll tell the police it was all an elaborate publicity stunt that went wrong."

Zach scowled, thinking about how he'd pressed the Silence Alarms button with his bare finger. "The hospital isn't going to just ignore losing a patient. They'll check the security tapes and realize your nephew *was* involved. If they run prints, they'll figure out who I really am, and at the very least I'll get kicked out of the academy."

"*If* they run prints. They won't if there isn't a crime. I'll show them I'm hale and hearty and tell them the man in the hospital woke up and left on his own but doesn't want to be identified. Don't worry, they'll drop the investigation, especially if I offer to pay back the cost of the rescue efforts and hospital bills. I hate to do this as much as you do, but there really isn't a better option. H.Q. will live to die another day."

Zach rolled his eyes at the pun. If he wanted, he could poke any number of holes in Seamus' logic, but now that the immediate problem of getting him out of the hospital had been solved, he just wanted to return his parents' car before his stepfather went ballistic.

Seamus squeezed his shoulder with the hand that shouldn't exist. "It was by no means your fault it didn't work out. You have my thanks for giving it a go."

"What about the money? Do I still get it?"

Seamus laughed as he opened the door. "H.Q's checkbook is in the car. If you don't mind waiting, that is."

Zach nodded eagerly. Even his stepfather wouldn't argue in the face of ten thousand dollars.

Once he was alone, he took the opportunity to do a little micro-meditation to calm his overtaxed mind. He rested his hands palm up in his lap, took several long, slow breaths, and stared incuriously out the front windshield towards the bay. After a minute or so, his attention was caught by the sight of a bird streaking towards the Explorer. It was Caw, who always seemed to know where to find him. Zach lowered the driver's side window and stuck his arm out, watching as the sleek black raven dropped his tail and tilted his wings to land gracefully on Zach's wrist.

"Sorry, Bud, I don't have any food on me."

Zach imagined he saw a reproachful look in Caw's shrewd blue eyes. The bird took several deliberate steps, walking up Zach's arm until he reached his shoulder. He then fluffed his feathers and settled down, leaning slightly against Zach's cheek.

Zach often wondered why Caw had picked him over Kevin, or even Lizbeth. Of them all, Zach had been the least tolerant of the bird, yet when the time had come to leave the UK after the Cataclysm, Caw perched on Zach's shoulder, dug in his claws, and refused to budge. Since then, Zach's intolerance had turned to a grudging affection.

He glanced over at Seamus to see what was taking so long. The shapeshifter sat in the driver's seat of the Lexus with a cellphone to his ear.

Caw captured Zach's attention again by rubbing his head under Zach's chin and making clicking noises with his beak, interspersed with soft gravelly squawks. Sometimes Zach was certain the bird was talking to him in raven-speak.

Then without warning, Caw flapped his wings and produced an ear-piercing series of distressed 'awk-awk' sounds. Zach was about to tell the bird to knock it off, but Seamus rapped urgently on the driver's side window before letting himself in. Caw launched himself out the window and flew off.

"We've got trouble," Seamus said. "Listen to this."

He tapped the screen of his cell phone and a woman began to speak.

"Seamus, it's Sophie. Tainie's been missing for four days," there was a distinct break in the woman's voice, "Whoever took her hasn't contacted me or made any demands, but I think they're watching me. I couldn't take a chance on calling before now and Caitlin's last phone number has been disconnected. I don't know what to do. Should I go to the police? Please, please help me...Oh, my God. There he is again – the man who's been following me—"

The message ended abruptly.

At least half a dozen questions came to mind, but maybe because Zach only had two hours sleep and was running on fumes, he asked irritably, "Why did you say 'we' have trouble? I don't know those people."

Seamus skewered him with a narrow-eyed look. "Any time one of our people is at risk of being exposed, it affects us all."

Zach looked away. "I'm not exactly one of you."

"True. I wouldn't have chosen you if I thought you were on their radar, but maybe that was a miscalculation. Perhaps Caitlin and I should have warned everyone involved with the drill ship – not just the full fae – that they should go into hiding."

"You weren't hiding at last night's big party."

"You know what I mean. H.Q. is not me, nor is he connected to me in any way. That identity is ironclad – or was. Last night may have put all that in jeopardy. Are you really so self-absorbed that a woman whose daughter has been kidnapped leaves you unmoved? A police officer is supposed to protect and serve, if I remember rightly."

"I never said I was unmoved. Does that Sophie woman even live around here?" Zach saw the answer on Seamus' face and continued, "Then how am I supposed to help? Is this the Guild?"

"We suspect it's MI6, which is equivalent to your CIA, although I wouldn't be surprised if members of the Guild are assisting them. And you can help in any number of ways, but that's not what I meant when I said *we* had trouble. Sophie and her daughter were hiding out under new names – fake identities Caitlin procured. I'll wager young Tainie was unable to stay away from her old life, and that's how they caught her. They would have undoubtedly scrutinized the identities she and her mother were using, and if they traced them to the source..."

"The source – you mean the person who forged them?"

Seamus nodded. "Caitlin's too smart to have given the forger her contact information, but she uses multiple identities."

Zach finally caught on to Seamus' meaning. If the MI6 interrogated the forger and the forger talked, then it didn't matter which identity Caitlin assumed; they would know about them all.

"So call and warn her," he said.

"I tried. Like Sophie said, her phone's disconnected."

"Is that a good sign or bad?"

Seamus stared down at the phone in his hand. "Impossible to say. She's either aware of the problem and ditched the phone and her identity, or – I don't want to think about the other option. Are you in touch with Lizbeth?"

Zach shrugged. "Just through email..." he trailed off as he recalled her last message to him. "She said she was going on a trip with Caitlin. Somewhere on the east coast." And if Caitlin was in danger, that put Lizbeth in danger, too. His heart sank.

"What about Kevin?" Seamus asked.

He shook his head. "Nah, we don't talk. The last email I sent him got bounced back. That was like a month ago."

Caw chose that moment to dive bomb the car, squawking madly as he flew down to within a few feet of the hood and zoomed over the top of them. Instinctively, Zach looked in the rearview mirror.

A patrol car had pulled up directly behind the Explorer, blocking their exit.

"Aaand now we've got company," he said.

Chapter Twenty-two

Dublin, Ireland

Even though Caitlin had just interrupted Kevin in the middle of a kiss, she barely glanced at Tara before telling him curtly, "Let's go."

"Uh..." he said, waving vaguely in Tara's direction, "This is, uh..."

Caitlin turned to Tara, and in a voice that sounded anything but apologetic, said, "So sorry for the rudeness, but we really must be leaving."

While most people would wither under Caitlin's dismissive gaze, Tara appeared unfazed. She gave Kevin a bland look and asked, "Is this one of them?"

Caitlin didn't give him a chance to respond. "One of whom?"

Kevin felt like he was watching a slow-motion train wreck from a seat in the caboose. Caitlin hadn't sensed Tara, probably because of the power emanating from the kernel in his pocket. It was all he could do to utter, "Caitlin, this is Tara."

Caitlin took a small step backward, a guarded look on her face. "You're...one of us. What's going on?" In an instant, her expression changed to one of hopeful astonishment. "*Lizbeth?*"

Kevin reached out to touch Caitlin's arm, shaking his head. "No."

The hope faded rapidly. "Who, then?"

When Kevin didn't reply right away, Tara heaved an exaggerated sigh. "For goodness sake, just tell her. No, I will." She stuck out her hand. "Tara Keane. Newly, um, I don't know, changed?"

Caitlin looked at Tara's hand like it was a snake. "Kevin," she said through gritted teeth. "What have you done?"

"It wasn't his doin'," Tara declared. "It was me. I took it from him when he was sleepin'."

Caitlin sucked in a quick breath and turned to Kevin. "She touched it?"

"Yes," he said. "And she knows what it is – for the most part. I'm sorry, it was really unavoidable...I just..."

For lack of the right words, and to keep Tara from knowing the full truth of it, he sent Caitlin a quick series of impressions: Bill showing up in the helicopter; Kevin shifting into a dog and getting shot; Tara, a stranger sick with leukemia, but willing to help him; and his going back the next day to find the kernel of biometal. He put special emphasis on the memory of Tara telling him she'd eaten the tainted chicken. Finally, he sent the image of having to hide out in the cairn and discovering Tara had taken matters into her own hands.

"I see," Caitlin said slowly. She turned serious eyes on Tara for a moment, and then pinched the loose fabric at the waist of the stained green coverall she was wearing. "You're about my size. Have you a change of clothes I might borrow?"

Tara, ever practical, simply nodded and grabbed the strap of her new backpack. Kevin watched with open mouth as they walked off towards the 'loo' together.

After several long seconds contemplating how he would never, ever understand women, he got up and trailed after them. For the next ten minutes he pretended to peruse the souvenirs at a stand nearby the restrooms. When they came out, Caitlin was dressed in one of Tara's new outfits – another pair of serviceable jeans and a long-sleeved brown shirt with a bulky black sweater over it. She had also changed her appearance to that of a young woman closer to Kevin and Tara's age. Her hair was short, black and spiky, face round and features plain, as most of Caitlin's incarnations were.

As they walked towards the zoo's main entrance, the two 'girls' linked arms like the best of friends.

"Where are we going?" he asked.

"To get Lizbeth back," Caitlin replied.

"Where is she?"

"I have no idea."

"How are we going to find her? Felicity's dogs?"

Caitlin stopped in her tracks. She stared off into the distance for a moment. "No. The people who took her have a way to prevent that from working. Which reminds me. Keep an eye out for anyone wearing a plain black baseball cap. They've lined them with iron."

"Iron?" Tara asked.

Their arms were still linked, and Caitlin pulled Tara closer in what looked to Kevin like a sincerely affectionate gesture. Caitlin said, "There's a lot you don't know. I'll try to fill you in, but it may be a bit overwhelming."

Tara smiled. "I've got hair on my head. *Real* hair, and I can make it any color I want. I can handle whatever else goes along with it. Trust me."

Chapter Twenty-three

Somewhere in England

Two men in grey uniforms and helmets stood at attention on either side of the door on the roof of the Facility. The men wore thick black vests, combat boots, and each held an automatic rifle. As Lizbeth was escorted past them into the stairwell, their presence only emphasized the hopelessness of her situation.

From the outside, the building seemed to be only one story, but she, Bill and the two agents went down three flights of stairs, which told her the bulk of the Facility was built underground. They entered onto a hallway with white walls, grey carpeted floors, and lined with evenly spaced doors like an office building. The agent-in-charge turned to Collins and said, "Why don't you go check on our other guest?"

Collins nodded and went left, while the agent-in-charge steered Lizbeth to the right with a firm grip on her elbow. She looked up at Bill with a question in her eyes, knowing he couldn't read her, but would still understand she wanted to know about this 'other guest.'

His lips thinned. "*I don't know who it is. They don't tell me everything.*"

More than just the mental words, she picked up the impression that he'd lost something; like he'd done something wrong and 'they' no longer trusted him.

The agent stopped at a door with a cipher lock attached to the handle and used his body to block Lizbeth's view as he punched in some numbers. Inside was a large room with white walls, ceiling and floor. The cabinets and tables, too, were white, and Lizbeth wondered if the lack of color was meant to represent or encourage cleanliness.

The countertops were cluttered with computer monitors and other equipment she couldn't identify. The room was occupied by about fifteen people, men and women in white lab coats. Nearly everyone turned to see who'd entered, but the fact that each of them was also wearing a black cap told her they already knew who to expect.

Their stares were avidly curious and clinical at the same time. There wasn't a beaker or Bunsen burner in sight, but this was clearly a laboratory, and she was the object of study.

A short, delicate looking man with thin grey hair sticking out from under his cap hustled over to them, rubbing his hands together eagerly. His eyes never left her face as he nodded in her escorts' direction and said, "Carlisle. Masters." He had a thick Scottish accent. "Ms. O'Connor. What a monumental pleasure. Do you happen to remember me?"

Lizbeth had a hard time keeping the panic out of her face, but she wasn't about to confess that of course she didn't remember him because she wasn't really Caitlin. She held tight to the belief that as long as they thought they had the real deal, they wouldn't be out there trying to catch her grandmother. If anyone could rescue her, it was Caitlin.

"Should I?" she asked in her imitation of Caitlin's voice and manner.

The man chuckled. "Well, it's been years and I've aged some, whereas you look exactly the same. Truly extraordinary."

She lifted her chin. "Perhaps your *name* would jog my memory."

"Och, I was hoping I'd impressed you enough tae remember, but it's Brendan Nesbitt...Professor Nesbitt from the University of Glasgow? You attended a seminar I taught on molecular genetics in the late eighties."

Lizbeth nodded, but blinked and glanced briefly down so he would think she was only being polite. To change the subject, she took a chance by saying, "The field has certainly changed since then."

Her deflection worked: Professor Nesbitt began what would have probably been a long-winded, one-sided discussion on the changes in the field of genetics if Carlisle, the agent-in-charge, didn't interrupt.

"Shouldn't you get started?"

Lizbeth stiffened up and held her breath for a moment, then looked at Bill. His response consisted of two words that chilled her to the bone: *"Blood samples."*

Professor Nesbitt had the grace to look contrite, but he waved her over to a high-backed chair with flat arm rests. She'd given blood a time or two when she'd been sick and recognized a phlebotomy chair when she saw one. It wouldn't do her any good to resist, so she sat, spine straight, trying to seem cool and detached. To emphasize her cooperation, she pushed up the sleeves of her sweater on both arms and laid her forearms on the rests, palm up. If anyone noticed her shaking hands, they didn't comment on it.

A gloved woman stepped forward, tied a rubber tube around Lizbeth's right arm, and wiped the crook of her elbow with a pad that smelled sharply of alcohol. Without a word, the woman methodically drew several tubes of blood, her touch light and impersonal. Lizbeth looked away the entire time, refusing to wince at the pain and maintaining a slight sneer on her face to show her contempt.

The woman removed the needle, taped a cotton ball to Lizbeth's arm, and handed the tubes to Professor Nesbitt, who looked at the blood samples as if he was surprised to see they were a normal dark red. He hesitated like he wanted to explain to 'Caitlin' what tests he was planning to run. A hard look from Agent Carlisle reminded him of his duty, and he muttered simply, "Good tae see you again, Ms. O'Connor," before walking away.

Agent Carlisle grabbed her arm and tugged on it, saying, "Let's go."

Bill stepped closer, his body language subtly threatening. "Give her a minute, would you? That was a lot of blood."

Lizbeth felt slightly nauseous and more than a little woozy, but she stood. "I'm fine."

Bill might be her only hope of getting out of here, and she didn't want him getting banned from her presence because he couldn't control his chivalrous urges.

They went back out into the hallway and turned in the direction Agent Collins had taken. Lizbeth took note of the regularly spaced camera domes in the ceiling. The room they entered looked nothing like the laboratory. The walls were still white, but the same grey carpeting from the hallway covered the floor. There were fabric-covered grey cubicles lining the left half of the room, most of them occupied by men and women dressed in the same uniform as the guards on the roof. Lizbeth decided they were soldiers, and like the lab techs, they all wore black caps.

The right half of the room had three office-sized, glass-fronted enclosures, each with a heavy security door. Two of the rooms were dark, but the third was lit from within. The walls and floor of the interior was covered with padded white material, like a holding cell for someone suicidal. Slumped dejectedly in the far-left corner was a young woman.

Agent Carlisle led her over to the cell. "It's a one-way mirror and bulletproof lead glass – so don't bother trying to contact her." He tapped his forehead a few times with his middle finger.

She stared at the girl, and it was all she could do not to laugh. There was nothing funny about the girl's plight, but her captors were trying to trick her and had no way of knowing it was transparently obvious.

The girl wore Lizbeth's face. She had the same light brown skin and black hair, but it was cut in the style Lizbeth had worn the year before: short and shaped in the back, tapering to longer strands in the front. Her captors must have shown whoever it was behind the glass Lizbeth's senior high school photo and coerced her, or possibly him, to shift into Lizbeth's form. Lizbeth didn't want to think about what they'd done to get the other shapeshifter to cooperate.

She glanced at Bill, but already knew from what he'd 'said' earlier that he was unaware they'd captured another one. He looked angry, though.

Agent Carlisle was watching her face to gauge her reaction. He said, "All we want is the crown and we'll let you both go."

Lizbeth did laugh then. "Well, that's a pity. If you'd bothered to ask Bill, he would have told you I'm dead set against anyone else becoming an initiate. The crown is gone. I destroyed it."

Chapter Twenty-four

San Francisco, California

Zach watched in his side-view mirror as the patrolman got out of his cruiser and approached the Explorer with his hand on his weapon. His first thought was that his stepfather had called the police and reported the SUV stolen, especially when the patrolman stopped several feet back from the open driver's side window and called out, "Keep your hands where I can see them!"

Zach's hands were already high up on the steering wheel, but out of the corner of his eye he saw Seamus raise his. In the mirror, Zach saw the patrolman glance around nervously as if he were hoping for backup. He was maybe forty, a small man with a soft belly that Zach could easily take if it came to that.

"What's the problem, officer?" Zach asked.

"License and registration," the patrolman said, taking a cautious step closer and loosening his gun in its holster.

Zach reached into his pocket, looking sidelong at Seamus, who said quietly, "Seem like an exaggerated response to you?"

"Something's got him spooked," Zach whispered back.

"I'll read him."

Moving carefully and keeping his hands where the patrolman could see them, Zach opened his wallet. He held his driver's license out and at the same time, leaned back so Seamus would have a direct line of sight. The patrolman took his license, squinted at it and then looked at Zach's face, taking his time.

"Ohhhh." Seamus' voice was barely audible. "He's stalling. There's an APB out for us. The feds are coming."

Zach produced a long, heartfelt sigh, wishing it hadn't come to this. If the feds were rounding up the folk and anyone associated with them, there was a good chance he'd never see Lizbeth again. If they knew what she was, she'd be locked up and studied like a lab rat. Tortured even.

With a heavy heart, Zach made his decision. There really was only one course of action.

When the patrolman bent down to hand the license back, Zach's right hand darted out and clasped his wrist. With a violent yank, he pulled the patrolman towards him, slamming his face into the edge of the car's roof while divesting him of his gun with his left hand.

The gun was a 9mm Glock, similar to the one Zach owned. Before he'd begun firearm training at the academy, he'd never touched a gun in his life. He'd gotten slightly above average scores on the proficiency exams – he could hit any given target with consistent accuracy – but had excelled in tactical training, specifically: disarming his opponent.

The patrolman was bent double, a hand to his bloody nose. Zach transferred the Glock to his right hand, opened the car door slightly, and before the stunned patrolman could straighten up, thrust the door outward. It connected with the patrolman's forehead with a dull thump, knocking him onto his backside.

Zach got out and trained the gun on the groaning patrolman, glancing in at Seamus, who looked perturbed.

"What?" Zach asked.

Seamus' eyebrows rose along with his shoulders. "Nothing. A bit excessive, maybe."

"You want to wait 'til the cavalry gets here?"

"Not at all." Seamus opened his door. "We'll take my rental. It's faster."

Zach looked around the parking lot, but it was nearly deserted and those people he did see were pretty far away and didn't look as if they'd noticed the altercation. He squatted down and pinched the plastic buckle on the patrolman's duty belt, which popped open and dropped to the ground. He removed the handcuffs from their pouch and pulled the unresisting patrolman to a standing position. Once he'd opened the back door of the SUV, it was a simple matter of shoving the patrolman inside face-down on the center seats and cuffing his hands behind his back.

The patrolman turned his head, leaving a dark streak of blood on the upholstery and spat, "You're gonna get your ass kicked for this, kid."

"Yeah, probably," Zach replied.

Before shutting the door, he reached into the patrolman's pocket to remove the keys to the cruiser. He didn't bother warning him not to move. It was a given that the patrolman would do everything possible to escape as soon as Zach left him alone. To ensure he wouldn't follow them or call for backup, Zach beeped the locks on the cruiser and retrieved the patrolman's duty belt from the pavement. Caw did another squawking flyby as he walked around the SUV and calmly got into the passenger seat of Seamus' Lexus.

"Where to?" he asked.

Seamus pushed the 'end' button on his cell phone with the thumb of his left hand and shifted into reverse with his right. "Airport. I've got H.Q.'s pilot on standby."

Chapter Twenty-five

Dublin, Ireland

Caitlin had been forced to steal a car at the airport, and they used it to drive the short distance to a parking garage near Trinity College. From there, they walked to the campus like any other group of students. The grounds were a blend of very old, ornate buildings offset by modern architecture. The wind had picked up and a dark bank of clouds moved rapidly overhead. It gave the campus an almost sinister atmosphere and Kevin felt a bit like he'd stepped into a Charles Dickens tale.

"So what are we here for?" he asked as they walked across an open area paved in worn grey bricks.

Caitlin kept walking, and for a moment he thought her old ways were going to assert themselves and she wasn't going to clue him in on her plans, but she said, "I learned something intriguing from an old schoolmate in the states and I'm looking for information. There's a professor here who might be able to verify it for me. His name is Marc Kim. He teaches astrophysics and is a bit of a character."

"Character? You mean like The Nutty Professor?" Tara asked.

Caitlin laughed. "No. He lacked a sense of humor as far as I could tell. Kim is a self-styled UFO debunker. Rather notorious for it, in fact."

A sharp breeze from behind blew Tara's golden mane into her face. She brushed it away, fingers lingering on the strands. "Is that what we're here to talk about? UFOs?"

"Not exactly."

"How do you know him?" Kevin asked.

"I took a few of his classes when I attended here some years ago – with a different identity, of course. Some of the students thought it amusing to disrupt his lectures with questions about alien encounters and such, which always sent him off on a tangent."

"I thought we were going to find Lizbeth," Kevin said.

"Yes, and as soon as it occurs to me exactly *how* to go about doing that, we will. Ah. There he is. Right on schedule."

An overweight Asian man of average height, wearing an open overcoat over a saggy tan cardigan was just leaving one of the newer-looking buildings. He had a laptop bag slung over his shoulder and was fiddling with his smart phone. He didn't notice Caitlin until he practically ran into her.

"Pardon," he muttered, stepping to one side without looking up.

"Professor Kim?" Caitlin said.

He stopped and turned, clearly disgruntled at the interruption. "What?"

"I'd like to talk to you about a recently intercepted message from space."

Kevin exchanged a surprised look with Tara.

The professor's jaw shifted forward in a pugnacious frown and he thrust a chubby finger into Caitlin's face. In heavily accented and broken English, he cried, "I know what you doing! So clever student. Administration ban me from discussion of UFO and now all student mock me and make special effort get me in trouble!"

He stalked off, but Caitlin called after him, "I'm a former student. I'm not here to trap you, I just want the truth."

Professor Kim stopped again. He looked Caitlin up and down and took in Kevin and Tara's appearance, too.

Caitlin didn't wait for him to dismiss her again. "I have it on good authority that a radio signal-"

"Not radio," Professor Kim interjected. "And we don't talk out here. Too cold. You buy lunch, we talk."

He waved for them to follow him and went back to his smart phone as they walked to a café off-campus. It was warm inside, and Kevin soon felt his chilled ears begin to thaw. They'd apparently beaten the lunch crowd and were quickly seated at a table near the window.

Tara sat next to Kevin, beaming as she took in the café's homey atmosphere. It occurred to him she'd lived her whole life on that isolated farm and wouldn't have gotten out much, especially after she'd gotten sick. Her life had taken an impossibly dramatic turn and was essentially just beginning. She must be experiencing everything, even a stop at an ordinary café, with a renewed sense of wonder.

The waitress bustled over, smiled at Professor Kim and asked, "Your usual, sir?"

He nodded absently, concentrating on removing his laptop from its bag.

Caitlin ordered a sandwich while Kevin and Tara, who'd eaten less than an hour ago, settled for tea.

After the waitress left, Professor Kim opened his laptop. He typed something, waited, and typed again. When he seemed satisfied, he looked up at Caitlin.

"What is your name?"

"Andrea Bower."

"I don't remember you." Professor Kim seemed mildly suspicious, so Kevin reached out with his gossamers only to determine that the professor *was* mildly suspicious.

"I was quiet. Sat in the back," Caitlin said.

Professor Kim snorted. "Where you hear about this message?"

"From a friend at STScI."

"Ah." Now she had his attention.

She pressed her advantage. "You said it wasn't a radio signal?"

He made a noncommittal face. "All I can say, message not picked up by radio *receiver*."

Kevin got an impression from the professor's mind of a large metal box, an experimental design of an electromagnetic machine of some kind. It had picked up an unusual repeating signal originating from beyond Earth's orbit. During the Cataclysm, over a thousand satellites had been sent crashing to Earth, but quite a few had also been sent spinning off into space. Professor Kim thought the signal in question was coming from one of those satellites.

Caitlin waited as the waitress set mugs in front of Kevin and Tara and filled their cups with hot water. After the waitress walked away, though, Professor Kim spoke again. "STScI is not interested in my opinion. They ask my colleague to analyze signal. Linguistics expert."

Caitlin leaned forward. "It's a verbal message?"

Professor Kim shrugged. "It noise to me."

"Do you have it? May I hear it?"

"Why your friend at STScI not let you listen?"

Caitlin smiled without a trace of humor. "Because he was asked not to share it."

"Smart move. Why encourage public to freak out over nothing?"

"You think it's nothing?"

He rolled his eyes and sarcastically emphasized each word, "Every sighting or encounter is hoax or has logical explanation."

"If the message isn't real, where's the harm in letting me hear it?"

"No harm. Surprised it not already on Internet, making UFO crazies happy." He turned his laptop towards her and pressed a key.

Kevin listened to the series of sibilant sounds, clicks and guttural noises in fascinated horror. During the fight to stop the Gossamer Sphere, his consciousness had traveled light years away to encounter and communicate with an alien mind. Somehow, he'd understood what the alien entity was 'saying' even though he'd never heard the language before.

The message on Professor Kim's laptop was in that language.

Kevin gasped and turned to Caitlin, who seemed to have been expecting his reaction.

She sent, *"What does it say?"*

With a chill running up and down his spine, he sent back, *"They're coming."*

Tara, unaware of what had passed between them, looked at Kevin and commented, "That sounds just like the weird language you were speakin' in your sleep."

Chapter Twenty-six

Somewhere in England

Lizbeth had no idea what Caitlin had done with the crown. She told Agent Carlisle it had been destroyed because he'd raised the stakes by threatening whoever it was behind the lead glass, and on the off chance he believed her, it would give him one less reason to keep her here.

"You destroyed it," he said. "And yet, from what I understand, the substance the crown is made of is virtually indestructible. How'd you manage it?"

Lizbeth was intimidated and got more so every minute she had to endure being held captive in this underground facility in the company of people who wanted, at the very least, to subjugate her. She was also angry. She wanted to lash out at Agent Carlisle, who thought he was her superior; thought he'd stumped her, caught her in a lie so poor she couldn't possibly think her way out of it.

But she held her tongue. Every step of the way since she'd taken on her grandmother's aspect, she'd asked herself: *What would Caitlin do? What would she say?*

With all the hauteur she could muster, she responded evenly, "I've been alive for two thousand years. I know things about this world a person such as yourself could only begin to guess. The crown is gone. It does not matter what you do to me, I cannot bring it back into existence."

Agent Carlisle sneered. "I don't believe you. I know what the crown can do. No one would be fool enough to destroy it. And please keep in mind we don't have to do anything to *you*." He tilted his head towards the glass-fronted room.

She stared in at her doppelganger, who still sat dejectedly in the corner, picking at the frayed fabric around a hole in her jeans.

Caitlin had entrusted Lizbeth with the crown after she'd been arrested the second time. Back then, the authorities weren't yet hunting them down and Lizbeth managed to keep it safe. She hadn't seen or heard of it since Caitlin took it back. Those months it was in her possession, though, gave her time to think about how best to dispose of it should it become necessary.

She shifted focus from the girl in the white room to her own reflection in the glass. Caitlin's beautiful face smiled, and she wished it really was her grandmother in front of her.

"I assure you, it's gone," she said. "It was the Cataclysm that gave me the idea – and the means – to destroy it." She looked at Agent Carlisle, letting her smile fade. "Have you heard of the Buzzard Creek Volcano? It's in Alaska. Before the Cataclysm, it hadn't been seismically active for thousands of years. That's where you'll find the crown. Of course, millions of tons of magma might put a damper on your search."

With startling swiftness, Agent Carlisle raised his hand, but Bill must have been expecting it, because he stiff-armed the agent before he could strike her. Agent Carlisle stumbled back into the glass, bumping it with his shoulder. Out of the corner of her eye, she saw the girl inside look up at the noise, but it was Agent Carlisle that had her full attention.

He smiled at Bill, a feral show of teeth. "I was hoping you'd do that." He backed off, looked over Bill's shoulder and nodded to someone. Two of the soldiers stepped over and took hold of Bill's upper arms.

"Isolation room one," Agent Carlisle said.

The soldiers started to haul Bill off, but the main door to the area opened and Agent Collins entered followed by three men. The newcomers all wore military garb and one of the soldiers detaining Bill immediately straightened up and said loudly, "At*ten*tion!" With a collective stomping of boots, every soldier in the room stood.

None of the newcomers' heads were protected. Agent Carlisle thrust his hand towards the cubicles and barked, "Hats!" but the man in the center stepped forward and said, "Not necessary."

Agent Carlisle looked almost apoplectic but didn't protest.

The man who'd spoken was tall, the same height as Bill, with reddish blonde hair greying at the temples. He took in the girl in the white room and the men holding Bill, frowned at Agent Carlisle and then looked straight at Lizbeth. "I have nothing to hide from our guest. Do you know who I am?"

Lizbeth reached out with her gossamers and found his name at the forefront of his mind. "You are Sir Marcus Hawthorne." The name and title meant nothing to her other than the obvious fact that he was high up in the British military.

"*General* Hawthorne, if you please. I'm told your name is Caitlin O'Connor and you are a shapeshifter and telepath." He said it without a trace of sarcasm or doubt.

Since General Hawthorne seemed to favor the direct approach, she asked, "What do you want with me?"

"According to Mr. Masters, you're responsible for the sudden cessation of the Cataclysm."

"I didn't do it alone." She glanced pointedly at the girl behind the glass. "And look at the thanks we get."

"Yes, well, some of those who know of your existence have quite naturally wondered whether you were responsible for setting it off in the first place."

"That's ridiculous!" Bill exclaimed, struggling to pull his arms loose from the grips of the soldiers. "I told you they had nothing to do with it!"

"Calm down," General Hawthorne said, nodding at the soldiers to release him. "I didn't say *I* thought so. It just happens to be one of many things we'd like to clear up. You were not terribly forthcoming about the *cause* of the Cataclysm, Mr. Masters."

"Even Caitlin didn't know everything about what was really happening." Bill straightened his jacket and turned to Lizbeth. "I had no choice but to tell them. After the scientists on the drill ship died, they threatened to charge me with negligence."

Lizbeth thought he would have gotten off easy with a negligence charge. Those scientists thought the ship's mission was to explore Silverpit Crater – they couldn't have known the consequences for not following protocol around the core samples. Caitlin had urged her not to judge Bill too harshly, though, reminding her that if Caitlin thought his methods would have succeeded, she too would have risked the scientist's lives to stop the sphere.

This was neither the time nor place to confront him with her opinion, however. All she said was, "Self-preservation can be an ugly thing."

General Hawthorne crossed his arms over his chest. "It sounds as if you're speaking from experience. Is it true you can never die?"

"I'm sure you know very well I can be killed. Agent Carlisle here was just threatening whoever it is you have in that room."

General Hawthorne gave Agent Carlisle a questioning look.

The Agent didn't deny it. "My direct superior told me to do whatever necessary to get the crown...*sir*." To Lizbeth, he asked, "How'd you know it wasn't her?"

"Um, well," Lizbeth said, stalling as she tried to think up a reason other than, 'Because she's me.' It took way too long for her to stutter, "I – my granddaughter hasn't worn her hair like that in over a year."

To cover for her fumble, she demanded, "Who is it?"

Agent Carlisle, with an almost insolent expression on his face, looked to General Hawthorne, who said, "Tell her. Tell her everything. We won't get her cooperation through threats."

"She said she destroyed the crown." Agent Carlisle said it like it was his ace in the hole.

General Hawthorne shook his head. "This is no longer about the crown."

That bold denial almost made Lizbeth laugh. It had always been about the crown, about finding out everything they could about her kind and taking control. Still, General Hawthorne had come before her without protection – a show of faith that couldn't be faked unless he had uncommon control over his own thoughts.

"You have to look into my eyes to read my mind, isn't that right?" He was staring at her, a clear invitation. His eyes were pale blue, with reddened, slightly yellow tinged sclera. She reached out with her gossamers once more, to discover, if she could, his true intentions.

He wasn't thinking in deliberate sentences like Bill; his purpose wasn't to communicate with her, but to allow her access to whatever was on his mind. She got several rapid impressions that told her he'd attended a top-secret teleconference with leaders from across the globe. Emotion was difficult to detect, but Lizbeth felt confident that tough and powerful General Hawthorne was frightened – more so than he'd ever been.

It was true he no longer wanted to subdue and control her kind. Now he simply wanted their help.

Chapter Twenty-seven

San Francisco, California

Somewhat to Zach's surprise, they made it to the highway with no sign of pursuit. He looked out the window, drumming his fingers on the armrest. He hadn't been to this section of town since before the Cataclysm. Much of San Francisco's transport infrastructure had been destroyed, so what would have been a short hop onto Highway 101 required several detours. The Sierra Point peninsula was gone, so they were forced to take Bayshore Boulevard, but that road led to the airport anyway – what was left of it. The airport, its buildings and roadways, had suffered significant damage. The southeastern section of runway, like Sierra Point, had sunk into the bay.

While they drove, he removed the extra clips from the patrolman's duty belt with the intention of hanging onto the gun, but Seamus said, "You'll need to leave all that behind. If we're boarded, we won't be able to explain it."

"Are we likely to get boarded?"

"Not unless the feds catch up with us."

Zach twisted around to look out the back window. Traffic was light. There were no flashing lights or any other indication they were being followed.

At the airport, all went smoothly. H.Q.'s jet was unmarked on the outside, no dings or smudges on the paint, and inside it was opulent, nothing like the one Caitlin had chartered when the Cataclysm first began. It seemed so long ago, yet it had been less than a year.

In the guise of H.Q., Seamus made a show of very slowly climbing the ladder to board. When they were halfway up, Caw appeared, zooming up from behind and landing on Zach's shoulder.

"He's not going to poop in my plane, is he?" Seamus asked.

"Maybe," Zach replied.

The jet had a pilot and copilot, but no crew. Seamus said the less weight they had on board, the faster they could get to their destination. Zach thought having a steward to wait on just them would have been pretentious anyway.

As the jet took off, Zach began to worry about the patrolman he'd left cuffed in the back of his stepfather's SUV. If it had been Zach lying there, he would have struggled to a sitting position to look out the window and get the license plate number of Seamus' car. Had he hit the guy too hard? Because one thing seemed certain: their getaway had been too easy. Police were thin on the ground all over the city, but when one of their own went down, they seemed to materialize out of thin air. The feds should have gotten there soon after Seamus drove off. Even if the patrolman was unable to break out of the SUV, they would have found him and called for backup.

Once the jet straightened out, Caw began to walk the immaculate carpet, exploring for nonexistent crumbs. Zach stayed seated in one of the luxurious cream-colored leather seats while Seamus moved to a couch across from him. "There's food and drink if you like, or you can nap."

"Where are we going?" It struck him then that he might be on the run for a very long time. A pang of homesickness blossomed in his gut.

"New York to refuel and then London," Seamus said.

"How long's that going to take?"

Seamus patted his seat. "She's fast and we're light on passengers. Fourteen hours?"

"You think Caitlin's in London?" *And Lizbeth*, he thought, hoping she was safe.

"You care about her very much, don't you?"

"Who, Caitlin?"

"No. Lizbeth."

Zach frowned. "What, were you reading my mind just now?"

When Seamus shrugged, Zach said, "Don't, okay? It's none of your business how I feel about Lizbeth or anyone else."

"I read everyone every chance I get. It's why I'm still alive."

Zach looked away, sliding down a bit in his seat. It was okay to relax now, but he couldn't. He was irritated at Seamus and worried about Lizbeth. Plus, the consequences of his actions, of attacking a *police officer*, were just beginning to sink in.

He was supposed to be one of the good guys. That patrolman had just been doing his job.

Zach sank farther down into the seat as Seamus got up and disappeared into a different section of the jet. Zach was tired and thought a nap would be a good idea, but he felt hyper alert, like even Seamus couldn't be trusted. Of course, the shapeshifter's confession that he habitually read everyone's mind was disquieting, but on the other hand, if he hadn't read the patrolman's mind, they'd be in jail by now.

Or would they?

When Seamus came back, dressed more appropriately for H.Q. Spencer in a pair of pressed slacks and a tan, buttoned sweater, Zach asked, "Why do you suppose the feds never showed?"

"We must have gotten a good start on them."

"Or you lied."

H.Q.'s thin white eyebrows rose. "Why would I do that?"

"Because you wanted me to come with you. Wanted a personal bodyguard you could trust."

Seamus laughed. "You *are* a smart one. I hope Caitlin changes her mind and lets you become an initiate."

"Is that an admission?"

"Of sorts. That phone call from Sophie changed everything. We're being hunted. *Lizbeth* is being hunted."

Zach shook his head, glaring at Seamus, who didn't seem the slightest bit remorseful. The fact that he kept mentioning Lizbeth, using Zach's feelings for her to get him to cooperate, made him furious.

"You said you picked me to pose as your heir because you could trust me," he said.

"I do trust you."

"Well, I'll tell you what. Maybe you could before, but not now. Can't trust someone who doesn't trust you back."

Seamus stretched H.Q's frail legs out into the aisle. "Oh, I'll win it back. I don't know how much you know about the folk, but some of us have abilities that even Caitlin's science can't explain. I *know* she's in trouble. You'll thank me eventually."

Zach thought about Kevin; how he'd often known bad things were going to happen right before they did. Zach had learned to trust that ability, but then again, Kevin had never used it to manipulate him.

"You're pretty sure of yourself," he said.

"If there's one thing I've learned after all my centuries on this earth, Zach, it's that human nature will win out. But even if I'm wrong – and I'm not – you aren't cut out for a beat cop's life. There are bigger things in store for you."

Despite his anger, despite the fact that he knew Seamus was still attempting to influence him, Zach felt a thrill of excitement. Combating the Gossamer Sphere had been the single most important thing he'd ever done. He'd helped save the world.

And denial wouldn't change anything. The life he'd rebuilt for himself in San Francisco was behind him now in more ways than one. Lizbeth was somewhere up ahead.

Chapter Twenty-eight

Dublin, Ireland

Professor Kim seemed gratified when Caitlin tossed some bills on the table and pushed her chair back. Kevin was no longer reading him, but the professor's relief that they were leaving was written all over his face. Despite getting a free meal and the opportunity to UFO bash, he'd barely tolerated their invasion of his lunch break.

Invasion.

The word sparked another wave of goose bumps down Kevin's spine. The message had been short and in no way indicated what the senders' intentions were. They'd given a time frame for their arrival that meant nothing to him because it wasn't based on Earth's system of time. For all he knew, they could show up in a month, a year, or the next sixty seconds.

He and Tara stood and grabbed their backpacks just as the waitress arrived with the professor's soup and Caitlin's sandwich. When she saw Caitlin was leaving, the waitress said, "Did you want this as takeaway?"

"No, thank you," Caitlin said. She nodded abruptly at Professor Kim and squeezed past him into the aisle.

Tara made an exasperated noise, plucked a napkin from the dispenser and wrapped the sandwich in it. At Kevin's amused look, she said, "What? People are starving. Besides, she'll want it eventually."

Outside, it had just begun to rain. Caitlin started walking as if she had a destination but headed away from the college and the parking lot where they'd left the stolen car. Kevin and Tara pulled the hoods of their jackets up to cover their heads, but Caitlin had only a sweater. By the time they arrived at a modest hotel several blocks away, she was soaked.

As they walked up to the counter, she told them in a low voice, "I've stayed here before. They'll accept cash as long as we leave a deposit."

115

Within a surprisingly short amount of time, they were ensconced in a suite with a kitchenette, two double beds and a pull-out sofa. Caitlin mentioned she was desperate for a shower and disappeared into the bathroom with Tara's last clean outfit.

Kevin stood in the middle of the room, shell-shocked, while Tara divested herself of her backpack and coat and adjusted the thermostat on the wall. Then she took the sandwich from her pocket and put it in the little refrigerator before coming back into the main room and standing before him.

"What is it?"

He shook his head and opened his mouth, but words failed him, and he closed it again.

"You look like a fish out of water."

When he still didn't respond, she sighed and reached up to hook her fingers under the straps of his backpack. He dropped one shoulder and then the other to make it easier for her to remove it. Once it rested on the floor next to the sofa, she unzipped his jacket and very efficiently removed that, too. With the jacket neatly draped over the arm of the sofa, she put her palms on his chest and pushed him backward until he was forced to sit on the bed.

He blinked up at her in surprise, but she said in a very maternal manner, "You need a nap."

"No." He grabbed her hand and pulled her down onto the bed next to him. "I'm okay, it's just – a lot has happened, and now..."

"Is Lizbeth your girlfriend?"

"What?"

"You're stuck with me, and it's not convenient. I understand that. I didn't mean to throw myself at you before."

"She – no. I don't have a girlfriend. That's not why I'm upset. It was the message."

"Was it from them? The aliens who turned the Earth into a satellite?"

"Yeah."

"Are they coming to visit?"

He let out a weak laugh. She made it sound like an invitation to tea. "Looks like it."

"Well, then. I dunno 'bout you, but I'd like to get on with things since there's no way of knowin' what our lives'll be like once the new overlords arrive."

Now his laugh was stronger.

Lizbeth and Tainie exchanged glances.

"*Do you know where we are?*" Tainie sent.

"*No idea.*"

It never occurred to Lizbeth to ask Agent Carlisle, or the soldiers for that matter, who stood at attention surrounding the girls, reminding her of the Queen's Guard with their expressionless faces. After about ten minutes of shifting her weight from foot to foot, she heard a faint buzzing voice coming from Agent Carlisle's cell. He opened the door and cautiously peered around it.

"Okay," he said, nodding to two of the soldiers, who took up positions on either side of the door in the corridor. Lizbeth and Tainie were ushered into the back of an auditorium of sorts.

The room was big, with at least a hundred seats arranged in concentric circles that slanted slightly down towards the open center circle. The seats faced a curved wall that had more than a dozen oversized video monitors mounted on it. The central and largest monitor was blank, but the other monitors were split into either four or six video feeds, most with one or more faces staring out at the crowd. The lighting was subdued, but she could see that nearly every chair was occupied, and even though nothing seemed to be happening, voices were hushed.

Agent Carlisle led them down the steps to a section of reserved seats near the front. He seemed to be trying to keep a low profile, but a group escorted by armed soldiers didn't just walk into a room unnoticed. Several people in the vicinity pointed them out and low murmurs spread outward until it felt like everyone in the auditorium was looking at them. Lizbeth felt a hand on her arm and looked over her shoulder at Tainie.

"*You get the feeling we're late to the party?*" Tainie sent.

Lizbeth sat next to Agent Carlisle. "*I get the feeling we're* crashing *the party.*"

Chapter Thirty

En route to London, England

It took around five hours to reach New York in Seamus' private jet. Zach had discovered his seat was electric and fully reclinable, with a heated back and a massager, too. The luxurious seat had finally lulled him to sleep, and he barely stirred when they landed to refuel. He didn't particularly feel like talking to Seamus anyway.

They'd been in the air for several more hours when Zach admitted he couldn't sleep anymore. His goal had been to remain unconscious throughout the entire flight, but even if his body cooperated, Caw didn't. The raven was hungry and determined to tell Zach all about it by pecking at him unmercifully.

He shooed the bird away and saw that Seamus was lying on the couch across from him, snoring lightly. Zach got up and wandered into the back of the plane, finding the cabin's touchscreen control panel and discovering the local time was 3:30 a.m. He used the lavatory, and then found a mini refrigerator in the galley with a variety of frozen meals in the freezer compartment. He selected one and put it in the microwave. In a cupboard, he spotted a box of crackers, which he opened and set on the floor for Caw. It was an act of petty revenge allowing the bird to go at the crackers and make a mess in Seamus' pristine plane, but Zach didn't care.

After scrounging up a bottle of water, he poured half into a bowl for Caw. He then sat at a small table with four bucket seats around it and ate his meal, looking out the window at the darkness. He'd gotten used to the noise of the jet engine, but it seemed to have gotten louder in the last few minutes. They couldn't be landing; they were an hour and a half away from their destination, so he was pretty sure they were still flying high above the cloud layer. The window partially reflected the dim interior of the galley and yet

124

he kept catching glimpses of what looked like lights beyond the wings of the jet.

A noise from the cabin alerted him and he leaned over to see the copilot urgently shaking Seamus awake.

Seamus let out a couple of old man snorts that quite suited his H.Q. Spencer personality and sat up. "Yes, yes, what is it, man?"

Zach couldn't hear what the copilot was saying, so he got up and walked closer to catch the tail end of it, "...escort us to Northolt."

"Fine," Seamus replied. "Follow their instructions meticulously."

"Yes, sir." The copilot disappeared into the cockpit.

Zach sat next to Seamus on the couch. The cushions were still warm from the shapeshifter's body.

"What was that all about?" he asked.

"The plane is being flanked by two of Her Majesty's Royal Air Force fighter jets. We've been ordered to fly to Northolt, a military station just north of Heathrow."

"The military now?"

"Yes, Zach, the military." Seamus ground the words out. "I *told* you we were being hunted. They know what we are and are now bringing all their resources to bear to capture us."

"What are we going to do?"

"What are we –?" Seamus leaned back in irritation. "What the bloody hell do you think we're going to do? We'll do whatever they tell us to! If we're lucky I can talk our way out of this, but don't count on it. Shapeshifting and mind reading are very handy abilities to have, but they don't help much in a fight."

Zach didn't say so, but he disagreed. If he could read any given opponent's mind, he'd be able to anticipate the next strike.

Seamus must have been trespassing on his thoughts again, because he said, "One-on-one is different. Nothing's going to help us against an entire army."

"What do you think they're going to do with us?"

"You, I don't know. You're not fae. Me?" He looked away grimly. After a moment of tense silence he said, "You want to know how I lost my arm? The Guild left me locked up in the Tower of London for fourteen years, chained to a wall; one arm, one leg. Then one day my leg iron fell off. Just fell right off. The locking mechanism had rusted through. At that moment, I realized there was only one thing standing in the way of my freedom."

"Your arm."

"Bloody right, my arm."

Zach thought about it for a minute. "You could jump out of the plane and turn into a bird."

"Don't think I haven't considered it." Seamus clapped him on the back. "But there's a good chance this lot would just shoot me out of the sky, and even if they didn't, I'm not going to abandon you to them. You wouldn't be here if it wasn't for me."

"You trying to win my trust back?"

Seamus gave him a lopsided grin. "How am I doin'?"

"Get me out of this alive and I'll let you know."

The jet fighters stayed with them until just before they landed, peeling away during their final descent. It was a rough landing, and Zach wondered if it was because the pilot was unfamiliar with the runway or stressed out because of the circumstances, or both. They didn't taxi very far before stopping. When he looked out one of the windows, he saw the headlights of about a dozen military vehicles moving into position to surround them.

"Seriously?" he muttered.

"Like I said," Seamus responded. "Not a fight we can win."

The copilot came into the main cabin looking spooked. "Captain wants you to know they radioed us to open the door slowly and come out with our hands up. Like we're criminals!"

Seamus waved an arthritic hand through the air carelessly. "This is clearly a mistake, but I urge you to cooperate fully. Don't give them any reason to suspect us further. They should have full access to the plane, of course. I can't imagine why, but they must think we're smugglers or terrorists or something."

Or something, Zach thought, and got a sardonic look from Seamus.

As ordered, the copilot opened the door and extended the airstairs. Wind and rain blew in, and Zach zipped up his coat. The copilot hung back as if he was afraid to be the first out, so Seamus tutted a bit and moved into the doorway. Despite the requirement that he keep both hands in the air, he kept one hand on the rail and took the stairs as slowly as one might expect from a one-hundred-year-old man. Zach followed, both hands held high and Caw clinging to his shoulder. The headlights from two trucks were trained on the jet, so it was difficult to see exactly how big their welcoming party was, but he saw more than a few silhouetted soldiers with their weapons trained on them.

When he reached the tarmac, Caw launched himself into the air and flew off.

126

Once the pilot and copilot had joined Seamus and Zach, one of the soldiers shouted, "Is that everyone who was aboard?"

"Yes," Seamus replied in a particularly high and shaky old man voice, blinking in the bright light. "What is this about?"

A man Zach pegged as an officer stepped forward. "Lieutenant Colonel Sheldon Paxton at your service. H.Q. Spencer, I presume? And which of your companions is Zach Wong?"

The officer's eyes went straight to Zach, so he assumed the man already knew. "Yeah, that's me."

Seamus straightened up proudly. "If you would be so kind as to tell us why we are being detained...?"

"My apologies, sir, but that information was not given to us. Our orders were to escort you and Mr. Wong to another location. Please come with us."

As if we have a choice, Zach thought.

Lieutenant Colonel Paxton joined them in an armored car that already had two soldiers seated inside. Three other vehicles followed as they rumbled off down the road. Zach and Seamus said nothing to each other, nor were they addressed by the Lieutenant Colonel. The trip took less than an hour, and their destination was a large brick building.

Zach thought the inside of the building was going to be a jail or a laboratory, but to his astonishment, it was a darkened auditorium full of people. He looked at Seamus, who shrugged, obviously just as confused as he was.

The last person Zach expected to see as they were led to their seats was Caitlin.

Chapter Thirty-one

Dublin, Ireland

To Kevin's dismay, in order to get to Simon's place in the East of England, they had to take a ferry across the Irish Sea. He'd always suffered from seasickness and hadn't been on a boat since Caitlin had sent him to convince Bill Masters to sabotage the drill ship some months ago. Today the sea was turbulent with the rainstorm that had only grown more intense with time. To make matters worse, they weren't able to catch a ferry to Holyhead, a much shorter journey than the one to Liverpool. He actually started feeling sick the moment he set foot on the gangplank.

Tara, on the other hand, was buzzing with excitement. As they took their seats, she said, "I love the sea! I wish I could live on a houseboat or sail a yacht around the world."

"You seem adventurous," Caitlin said. "I'll wager you'd enjoy being a dolphin."

Tara's eyes went wide and then she grinned. "Or a seal. My mum's family name is Selkie."

"Really?" Caitlin sounded impressed. "You know, of course, the legends behind the name?"

Tara's head went back. "Are they *true*?"

"Well, the stories have been elaborated upon over the centuries as you might imagine, but many stories involving shapeshifters are true at their core. Before the Roman invasion of Britain, the Selkie family lived on the Orkney Islands. They were farm folk, prosperous enough, but not well to do. There were sixteen children, most of them girls with large brown eyes, but otherwise not beautiful. Their father could not marry them all off, so two by two he sent them on the long journey to Anglesey to become initiates."

"Initiates...that's shapeshifters, right?" Tara asked.

Caitlin nodded. "Tragically, all but three of the girls died. Which was good odds, actually, since most did not survive initiation. The Selkie girls made very effective druidesses. They were spies, you see, spending many an afternoon soaking up the sun as seals. They would cross the Menai Straight and boldly frolic at the feet of the Roman Legion, which was preparing to invade."

Tara had been listening with rapt concentration. "The stories I've heard were usually romantic."

"Ah, yes." Caitlin looked out the rain streaked window. "Romantic tragedies, most of them. I can't speak to the origin of those stories, just the one I know."

"Tell me more."

"The Selkie girls learnt much from the soldiers who spoke of battle strategy within their hearing, but one of them did not limit her spying to the beach. Morag was her name, and she was bold. Many of the local girls, you see, had been forcibly taken from their villages to attend the officers. Morag rescued one girl, spirited her away and then took her place to spy on the captain of the battalion. The night before the attack, the Roman soldiers killed every last one of those village girls. Morag barely escaped, and with the captain hot on her heels, ran for the ocean. The tides of the Menai Straight are treacherous, and the captain laughed to see her floundering in her skirts. He did not laugh long, for Morag shifted into a seal and swam away."

"Wow," Tara said. She turned to Kevin. "Did you know about that?"

Kevin swallowed bile and croaked, "No."

"Are you okay? You look green."

Without a word, he jumped up and rapidly traversed the main aisle to the head, where he threw up the soggy sandwich he'd eaten not an hour ago. When he returned, Caitlin was still answering Tara's unending questions. He listened to the answers, which helped distract him from the nausea, but he was very grateful when the ferry pulled parallel to the dock.

Night had long since fallen by the time they reached the abandoned Victorian farmhouse, driving across Great Britain in yet another stolen car. When they got out of the car, Kevin carried the duffle bag and one of the sleeping bags, while Caitlin and Tara brought the other two. They didn't bother going into the dark house, just walked around and headed straight for the grove.

The one streetlamp on the lonely road was dim and faded fast as they left it behind, and even though Caitlin had come prepared – distributing small but powerful flashlights to each of them – the darkness swallowed

129

everything. The flashlights did a great job illuminating the heavy, slanting rain, but failed to reach the sodden ground. Caitlin and Tara must have been nearly blind, but Kevin had excellent night vision. He took their arms and followed his senses towards the grove, escorting them through the wild grass. As he walked, he tried not to think of Wolfdogge and the three dead men they'd left here at the height of the Cataclysm. Their bodies were long gone, taken away by the police, who were never able to identify Brian Griffey, Kevin's real father.

The wind howled among the branches of the oaks, and the rain streamed down the trunks, carving rivulets in the mulch between the thick, abundant roots. He took a deep breath, inhaling the sweet scent of the earth and holding it in his lungs.

"This way!" he said cheerfully, helping Caitlin and Tara up and over the roots. When he reached their destination, he directed his light down into the black hollow at the convex of two huge roots. Caitlin knew where they were going, but Tara pulled back against his hold on her arm.

"In there?" she asked. "Are you kidding?"

Kevin had to agree it didn't look inviting. The last time he'd been down in the natural cavern formed by the roots of the oaks it had been moist, but not overly saturated. They were definitely going to get wet and muddy. Still, Caitlin was dead set on doing this and doing it *now*, so he asked, "You're not afraid of a little mud, are you?"

Under the beam of his flashlight, Tara's face scrunched up. "No, but that looks like a *lot* of mud to me!"

"Well, if I got on a boat in a storm, you can go in cave in a storm!"

"How is that the same thing?" she was shouting over the wind now.

In his mind, he heard Caitlin. "*The faster we do this, the faster we get out of the weather.*"

Tara must have heard her, too, because she stopped arguing. She did, however, give him a mocking smile and waved towards the opening. "After you!"

He ducked inside and looked around. Tightly woven roots formed the ceiling of the cavern, with several braided columns scattered throughout to support it. He looked down. If memory served, the ground was approximately ten feet below him, and from the looks of it, it wasn't just saturated, it was partially flooded. The water couldn't be any deeper than a foot or two, but there was no telling what was under the surface. A sharp stick could do major damage if any of them landed on it wrong.

There were no knobs or anything else he could use as hand holds on the roots that formed the entrance, but a yard or so in front of him was a

130

vertical, sturdy-looking root about the same thickness as a playground pole. Kevin had been no gymnast in school, but the root gave him an idea. He slung the duffle bag across his chest, handed Tara his flashlight and rolled his pants up to above his knees. Then he took off his boots and socks.

"Goin' wadin' are we?" Tara asked. It occurred to him that her sarcastic protestations were her way of dealing with the unknown, a lot like Zach. Kevin realized for all Tara's bold talk of adventure, she hadn't been anywhere or done anything exciting. Certainly not on the scale of what she'd been confronted with in the last two days.

He put a reassuring hand on her arm briefly before turning back to the entrance and shifting. He felt his nose shrink, arms and fingers elongate, legs shorten, and his pelvis and ribcage expand. When he was done, he dug his newly prehensile toes into the mud.

"Are you...?" Tara thrust her face towards him and squinted in the darkness. "Did you turn into a *monkey*?"

Kevin laughed and tried to tell her he was a chimpanzee, but it came out sounding like a series of demented grunts interspersed with gasps. Tara recoiled in fright, which only made him grunt and gasp louder. When he got himself under control, he sent, "*And* that's *what a chimpanzee sounds like when it laughs.*"

Tara recovered her equilibrium quickly enough and seemed ready with a comeback, but Caitlin sent, "*Let's do this, please.*"

Kevin grasped the pole-like root with his strong left hand and swung forward, surprised at how easily his shoulder and arm accommodated his body weight. He caught sight of another sturdy-looking root and reached for it. Soon he'd swung his way across the roof of the structure and spotted a section of raised ground on the far side that looked dry.

He dropped the duffle bag and swung back to the entrance, presenting Caitlin with his back. "*Get on. I got this.*"

She climbed on and clung silently to his shoulders as he efficiently made his way back to the patch of clear ground.

"*Ah, good,*" she sent, shining her flashlight around. "*This is perfect.*"

Tara, too, gamely got onto his back, but unlike Caitlin, let out a little shriek of panic each time he swung from root to root. When he dropped her next to Caitlin, he thought she was going to kiss the ground. He made three more quick trips for the sleeping bags and his boots.

Caitlin had laid her sleeping bag out by the time he shifted back into himself. He pulled his socks onto his frozen feet and unzipped his bag, sitting on the waterproof, cushioned fabric so he could roll his pant legs back down. Tara took off one shoe at a time and stuck her feet into the

131

opening of her bag before her socks touched the slightly moist, spongy ground. She stood there, head back, clutching her shoes and the neck of the sleeping bag in one hand, while running her flashlight beam over the roots that made up the roof.

"Um...maybe now's a good time to mention I'm right terrified of spiders," she said.

"I'm not fond of them myself," Caitlin replied. "Two thousand years and you'd think I would have overcome that particular prejudice."

"Can I put my shoes in the duffle bag?" Tara asked. "So nothing crawls into them?"

Caitlin held the bag open for her and she tossed them inside. "You know," Caitlin said, "the sleeping bags are not only waterproof, but they have pouches made of netting you can zip around your head."

Her voice hadn't finished echoing in the cavernous space before Kevin heard the sound of Tara's enthusiastically pulled zipper. He, too, zipped the netting around his head, not unhappy to be sealing out the multitude of creepy crawlies that were undoubtedly inhabiting the space they'd invaded. He idly hoped for Caitlin and Tara's sake that the aliens weren't arachnid-like creatures.

"I heard that," Caitlin said. "Now go to sleep."

He lay back, chuckling. The sleeping bag's insulation kept the twigs and rocks on the ground from poking him too bad, but he was aware of them nonetheless. Still, it was more comfortable than the cairn. There he'd gone to sleep on a frozen stone, looking up at the triskele symbol carved into the lintel...

Chapter Thirty-two

London, England

Lizbeth watched with open mouth as Zach, a very old man who looked vaguely familiar, and another bunch of soldiers filed into the row ahead of them and sat. Zach put his arm on the back of the seat and turned around, but one of the soldiers with him said, "Eyes front please."

In her mind, she heard, "*Hello, Caitlin. Have you any idea what this is all about?*"

"*Zach?*" she sent, shocked that she'd heard him.

"*No, it's me, Seamus.*" The old man in front of her lifted his hand, and she filed away the fact that Seamus didn't have to make eye contact to use his gossamers.

"*What are you doing here? Why is Zach with you?*"

"*Long story. I'm glad to see you found Tainie.*"

"*I didn't actually find her. We were brought together. And I'm Lizbeth, not Caitlin.*"

She heard the old man in front of her chuckle. "*Why am I not surprised? Where is our esteemed leader?*"

"*I don't know. She got away when they caught me.*"

"*So what is the point of this dog and pony show?*" Seamus' hand lifted again, and he waved it to indicate the auditorium.

"*All I know is this place is some kind of central command and the British military thinks they need us.*"

"*Do they now?*"

The internal conversation ended when General Hawthorne carried a microphone stand into the center ring, set the stand down, and held his hands up for attention. The crowd quieted quickly.

"Thank you all for coming. If you will please be seated and mute your personal communication devices, we will begin. I would also like to

133

take this opportunity to remind you that these proceedings are confidential, concerning matters that would greatly disturb the general public were they to be disseminated without careful foresight.

"We acknowledge the presence of the members of the UN Security Council, as well as many international heads of state and agency representatives both in person and via video consult, but we're going to have to skip the usual introductions so we might devote all of our time here today to the subject at hand. First on the agenda is a joint update from NASA and the European Space Agency."

Applause trickled through the audience as a thin, balding man with glasses and a heavyset blonde woman came forward. The woman took the mike as the man pointed a handheld device at the wall of monitors and the middle screen was filled with first the NASA logo, then the ESA logo, and finally an image of the starry night sky.

"Good morning," the woman said in an American accent. She seemed nervous to Lizbeth, like she wasn't used to speaking in front of a group. "I'm Stella Matthews, NASA, and this is Terrance Blount from the ESA. We've been asked to keep this short and to avoid getting technical, so we're going to show you what we have and then take questions. Several weeks ago, as I understand most of you already know, a signal from beyond our solar system was intercepted. In an effort to identify the source, Hubble Space Telescope, along with a few of the larger ground-based telescopes and antenna arrays that survived the Cataclysm, were oriented in the signal's direction. Data has been streaming in ever since.

"The following is a series of photographs of that region of space." Lizbeth could sense the woman's almost apologetic excitement, as if she knew what she was about to show them would confirm something...frightening.

Mr. Blount wielded the clicker importantly, allowing each photograph to stay on the monitor for about five seconds before going on to the next one. The pictures were all similar but of differing quality, and Lizbeth began to recognize the pattern of the stars, except for a glaring inconsistency that began to appear after the first twenty or so photos. Three of the stars appeared to be getting brighter and brighter as the slideshow went on.

"As you can see in comparing the earliest images with the most recent," Ms. Matthews said, "the central three equidistant bright points were not visible until forty-eight hours ago. They increased in brightness until seemingly disappearing from that region of space entirely."

A murmur rose from the crowd. Mr. Blount leaned down to the mike and in what sounded to Lizbeth like a Swedish accent, said, "Please hold your questions."

When the crowd had quieted again, Ms. Matthews went on. "Subsequent radar images from Goldstone confirmed that the bright objects, although no longer bright, had not disappeared, but had, um, in fact..." she trailed off and made a face like she didn't know how to continue. She nodded to Mr. Blount, who clicked to the next visual and completed the sentence for her, "Entered our solar system."

The black and white picture was grainy but showed what was obviously *not* an asteroid or comet or any other naturally occurring celestial body. Although Ms. Matthews had indicated there were three of them, the picture was of just one object, an oblong, mechanical structure. On one side was a design, three spiral circles that Lizbeth instinctively knew represented the triskele galaxies. The alien home world.

After a moment of stunned silence, the crowd exploded. People jumped out of their seats and shouted questions. "What is that?" "My God, it's a *spaceship*!" "Are they coming to Earth?" "What did the message say?"

The formerly placid faces on the video monitors surrounding the central monitor looked distorted, their mouths working, but no sound came out of the audio.

General Hawthorne stepped back into the ring and held his hands high in an attempt to get the crowd's attention. "Please remain calm!" he shouted. The chaos showed no sign of abating, so he grabbed for the mike. "Please take your seats so we may continue!" Even amplified, his voice could barely be heard over the noise of panicked people. It occurred to Lizbeth that if this was the reaction from the people in charge, what would the average person do?

She and Tainie, Zach and Seamus, Agent Carlisle, and every one of the soldiers just sat in their seats as the general continued to entreat the crowd for silence. Agent Carlisle leaned close to Lizbeth. "You don't look surprised."

"Bill really didn't tell you very much, did he?"

"He told us the metal the crown was made from was of alien origin." He nodded in the direction of the video monitors. "I'm willing to bet it was *those* aliens."

"That does seem to be the logical assumption."

He gave her an incredulous look. "You're going to sit there and pretend you didn't know about this?"

She sighed. He really was a jerk. "How was I supposed to know?"

135

His eyes narrowed and he held his head very still. "They're *your* people, aren't they?"

Chapter Thirty-three

London, England

Even though Zach knew about the Gossamer Sphere, knew Kevin had communicated with an alien entity, he was still shocked at the sight of the spaceship. Kevin had identified the triple galaxy as the alien's location – at least, the alien *he'd* talked to. The photos from NASA, however, didn't seem to be showing that distinctive galaxy, which meant the signal hadn't come from the same location. Once Zach thought about it, it made sense. The Gossamer Sphere had been sent hundreds of millions of light years away from the alien home galaxy to establish a communication satellite here on Earth. It was logical to assume they'd sent out many more, and with satellites all over the universe, there would also have to be civilizations using those satellites. Not to mention the fact that the sphere hit Earth sixty-five million years ago. How many civilizations had come and gone between then and now?

But even if the spaceship or ships lurking at the edge of Earth's solar system came from somewhere closer than the triple galaxy, the difference in light years couldn't account for how quickly they'd gotten here. *Faster than light travel*, he thought. Another example of science fiction proving itself to be science fact.

The meeting moderator was slowly gaining control over the crowd, entreating them to keep in mind that they were setting an example for their people, and they should behave accordingly.

Zach heard the guy behind him say something to Caitlin, and even though he couldn't make out the words over the noise, the contempt in the man's tone carried. Zach turned in his seat to glare at him, and this time when the soldier next to him said, "Eyes front," he ignored him.

In his mind, he heard Seamus say, *"You might care to know that's not Caitlin, it's Lizbeth."*

137

"Lizbeth?" Zach said, astonished. She turned to him with a grimace that said more clearly than words he was going to blow her cover, although why she was posing as Caitlin, he couldn't imagine.

She covered for his gaffe by saying, "She got away."

"Oh...right. That's good." He faced forward again, fighting several conflicting urges. He wanted to punch someone, of course. The soldier next to him was a good candidate, but the guy who'd disrespected Caitl – *Lizbeth* – was next on his list. He kind of wanted to cry, like several of the people in the audience around him. He already knew the people of Earth weren't alone in the universe, but it was one thing to know and another thing entirely to be on the verge of meeting a star-faring race. The very concept had yet to fully sink in. Most of all, though, he wanted to jump over the seat and take Lizbeth into his arms and tell her how he felt about her.

He almost did; almost said 'to hell with it' and threw caution to the wind, but the crowd finally quieted down enough for the moderator to open the floor to questions. For the next hour or so, the NASA and ESA representatives tried to answer them. Most of their responses began with the phrase, 'We don't know.'

When it seemed that the audience members had exhausted their questions, the speeches began. The British Prime Minister had arrived at some point, and got up to deliver an impassioned, and clearly impromptu, speech about cooperation between the countries of the world so they could show a united front. He and his entourage left immediately afterward. Not long after that, the man sitting in front of Zach showed his cell phone to the woman next to him, and Zach heard him say, "Looks like word is out."

Video feed suddenly appeared on the main monitor. The President of the United States was addressing the people. Stay calm, he said. We made it through the Cataclysm, we can handle this, he said.

Zach had the impression all along that this was supposed to have been a secret meeting for the heads of state to figure out what to do, but that had to have been a pipe dream. Something as big as this couldn't be kept quiet for long. After the president's speech, which, unlike the prime minister's, had obviously been carefully scripted for him, the meeting began to break up.

The emotions of the people nearby were a mixed bag: many were frantic, many more seemed stunned. All around him was the buzz: what to do? What to do?

He had the same question. Turning in his seat again, he addressed the freckled man sitting next to Lizbeth, who seemed to be in charge. "What are you going to do with us?"

138

In a morning chock full of overwhelming revelations, it still managed to surprise him when the man stood, climbed up onto his seat, pulled a weapon from his shoulder holster and fired up at the ceiling. Immediately following the blast, screams rent the air, and nearly everyone in the auditorium ducked down as if a giant unseen hand squished them to the floor. The soldiers reached for their weapons but stopped when the man swung his pistol around and pointed it at Lizbeth's head. Zach's blood went cold.

"This meeting is *not* over!" the man shouted, his voice filled with fury and fear. The tendons on his neck stood out as he struggled to hold his gun arm steady. "Everyone is acting as if we're helpless! Like sitting ducks waiting for these aliens to come to Earth and do what they want with us! But we've got a bargaining chip *right here*." He emphasized the words 'right here' by jabbing his gun in Lizbeth's direction. Then he glared across the seats toward the moderator. "Isn't that right, General Hawthorne?"

Chapter Thirty-four

East of England

Kevin woke on his back with his mouth open, a position he often found himself in first thing in the morning. He reached up to pull the sheet away from his face but encountered resistance. He swatted at the fabric, which seemed glued to his head, before remembering he was in a sleeping bag and the fabric was the netting at the opening.

He unzipped the netting and lowered the zipper along the side of the bag before sitting up. Caitlin and Tara were nearby, both just beginning to stir. It was still dark in the cavern, but the muted light of dawn was trickling in through the entrance.

He had the feeling something was going to happen, something momentous. He tried to recall if he'd dreamed, if the aliens had contacted him, but couldn't.

"Caitlin?" he whispered.

"I'm awake."

"Did they...?"

"Yes." She sat up and unzipped her bag. "They did."

"So what happened?"

"I think you will remember if you try."

He wanted to tell her he'd already tried but stopped himself. He was hungry, which made him irritable. He hadn't eaten since yesterday's soggy sandwich, and that hadn't stayed down long. He shouldn't take his frustration out on Caitlin.

And he *did* want to remember. He wished he had Zach's knack for relaxation, but he'd never had the self-awareness or self-control or whatever it was Zach used to put himself into a trance so easily.

Then he thought of the kernel in his pocket. It was nearly identical in size to the bit of biometal he'd removed from the drill ship core sample.

He'd heard strange hissing voices whenever he touched that bit of biometal, voices which turned out to have been snippets of the messages flowing through the Gossamer Sphere. He'd also had that bit in his hand when he'd spoken to the entity the first time.

He found the kernel at the bottom of his pocket and pulled it out, pinched between forefinger and thumb. He felt its power, but didn't hear anything, which made sense since the Gossamer Sphere had been shut down. It was no longer using Earth's magnetic field to relay messages for the alien beings. So how had they contacted him in his dreams?

He turned his head and looked at the nearest oak root.

A place of power, Caitlin had said. Access to the biometal grid deep in the lithosphere. Whether it was functioning or not, the biometal that made up the sphere had the power to boost his mental signal.

He wasn't prepared to talk to them again, not while he was conscious anyway. In fact, he shied away from the very idea, which might explain why he was having trouble remembering his 'dreams.' He took a deep breath and let it out slowly, like Zach always did. Another deep breath and he told himself, *Remember*.

He placed his hand on the root and closed his eyes. Just like the last time he'd 'communed' with the trees, as Caitlin put it, he felt a wondrous presence that was almost too much to bear. It was like and yet unlike the finest of sensations: the sweetest taste, the purest sound, the slaking of the deepest thirst.

He pulled his hand away, worried that he'd gotten too caught up in the experience. Sure enough, what felt like only seconds had been much longer. Caitlin and Tara were waiting, shoes on, sleeping bags rolled up.

"Do you remember?" Caitlin asked.

He started to shake his head, but then realized he *did* remember.

"They wanted to learn about us. Our language, customs, history."

Caitlin nodded. "So they don't come in blind."

But there was something else he'd picked up from them, something almost intangible, as if they hadn't meant him to know.

A warning.

Caitlin looked into his eyes, acknowledging that she'd sensed it, too.

"They're almost here," he said.

"Yes. We need to get moving. Find Lizbeth."

Kevin shook off the lingering feeling of, he didn't know what else to call it but 'rapture,' and shifted into chimpanzee form to take their belongings up to the surface. The storm had abated, leaving only a thick morning mist. There was no sun, of course.

141

They plowed through the wet field, songbirds serenading them all the way back to the stolen car – which was no longer the only car in the driveway. A silver Ford Focus was parked next to it, and a tall man in a trench coat leaned against the driver's side door.

When they got close enough, Caitlin demanded, "Where's Lizbeth?"

"Caitlin?" he asked. She looked nothing like herself, but Bill must have recognized her voice.

"Yes. Where is she?"

"She's safe," Bill said. "They haven't hurt her."

"How did you find me?"

"Well, first of all, your message was a bit of a shock, since Lizbeth is quite convincingly pretending to be you, but I've been up all night going to every place I thought you might go – at least the places the MI6 aren't already monitoring."

Caitlin took in a breath and Kevin couldn't tell if she wanted to laugh or cry. She said, "Where *exactly* are they holding her?"

"I don't know. They moved her." At Caitlin's doubtful look, he said, "I wouldn't lie to you – you'd just read my mind. They didn't tell me where they took them. I've been persona non grata since they found out I hadn't told them everything."

Caitlin let her duffle bag fall from her shoulder. "You told them enough."

"What do you mean, where they took *them*?" Kevin asked.

Bill's gaze didn't waver from Caitlin's face, as if he was searching for some sign of her real features. "Another shapeshifter. A girl named Tainie."

Kevin turned to Caitlin and she sent, "*Yes. Your sister.*"

To Bill, she said, "They're rounding us up."

"Oh, definitely. But not everyone thinks you're the enemy. These agents from MI6 would do anything to get their paws on the crown, but yesterday a military general showed up and threw a monkey wrench in their plans."

"A general?" Caitlin asked. "Was his name Hawthorne by any chance?"

"How'd you know?"

"His family were fae; one of the families I kept track of over the years. I considered approaching him to ask if he would help me stop the Gossamer Sphere but decided against it because his loyalties lay with the queen. This cannot be a coincidence. If General Hawthorne was raised on the lore, he may be an ally."

Kevin wasn't sure why Caitlin was telling Bill this; why they hadn't already left him standing in the dust of their leaving. Except...he still had the feeling something was very wrong. It gnawed at him worse than his hunger.

"Get in the car," Bill said. "I'll take you wherever you want to go. Don't argue. You know you're taking a foolish chance driving around in a stolen vehicle."

Kevin expected her to decline, but she simply said, "Thank you."

Kevin piled their gear into the back of the Focus. He took one last look at Simon's dilapidated old house. In the distance, a raven's raucous cry echoed over the landscape, reminding him of Caw and the day they found the crown. He shook off a feeling of melancholy and got inside the car.

Bill started the motor and turned to look back at Tara. "You look cold. Shall I crank the heater?"

Tara's arms were wrapped around her middle. "Yes, please."

Bill smiled. "We haven't been introduced. I'm Bill Masters."

"Tara."

Kevin noticed Tara didn't offer her last name. Essentially, she was a runaway. She was right to be careful, especially since Bill didn't exactly have a good track record keeping things to himself.

Bill didn't say anything further, just backed out of the driveway and drove down the road. When they got to the nearest town, Caitlin requested they hit a drive-through fast food restaurant. Bill accommodated her, even going so far as to pay for the overpriced, low quality food. Kevin chowed down two egg and sausage sandwiches and guzzled his orange juice. In the seat next to him, Tara ate her breakfast burrito with equal gusto.

As they drove towards London, Kevin couldn't escape the notion that something dire had happened or was going to happen soon. The impression was strengthened by a few odd sights out his window: thick black smoke rose into the air to the north, reminiscent of the fires that had been set during the riots at the height of the Cataclysm. And more than one car on the road was speeding, the drivers weaving in and out of traffic erratically. When he finished eating, he asked Bill to turn on the radio and tune to a news channel.

Bill pressed a button and they listened to the broadcaster for a few minutes, trying to make heads or tails of what he was talking about since they'd caught him in the middle of a sentence. Then the announcer said, "For those of you just tuning in, we're going to rebroadcast the prime minister's speech and have another listen to what the US president thinks as well."

They listened as two of the world's most powerful leaders spoke solemnly of a message from deep space and radar images of what could only be space-faring vehicles at the edge of the solar system.

"Oh, my God," Bill murmured. He glanced at Caitlin. "Did you know about this?"

"We heard the message. We knew they were coming."

"Of course," he said. "The sphere. Do you know what they want?"

Caitlin looked over her shoulder at Kevin.

He shook his head slowly. "No idea."

Kevin said it, but it wasn't entirely true. When he thought about it, he found he knew things about them that surprised him, like the fact that they weren't just one race; it was a consortium of intelligent species from many different planets. The ancient race that sent the gossamer sphere to Earth in the first place, however, was long gone. The civilizations that followed had inherited the technology, and the current administrators of the communication system linking colonized space had been horrified to discover humanity was occupying one of the satellite planets. Kevin was glad to know they were capable of the kind of emotions experienced on Earth.

Caitlin was still looking at him. "*The sphere came here, but Earth was not the original target, as I've suspected for some time.*"

He nodded. "*The ancients were targeting planets that couldn't sustain life. It was a fluke that the sphere was diverted here. I think...that's what the aliens are interested in. More than their curiosity about our world, they want to study what the biometal did to us.*"

Chapter Thirty-five

London, England

Lizbeth turned her head so she wouldn't have to stare down the barrel of Agent Carlisle's gun. The acrid odor of the spent bullet burned her nose. Zach was one of the few people in the vicinity who hadn't ducked down. He held her gaze and she clung to the sight of him like a lifeline.

General Hawthorne walked slowly up the aisle with his hands held up in front of him. "Put the gun down, Carlisle. We're all stressed out here. Everyone's emotions are stretched pretty thin."

"Oh, I'll put it down," Agent Carlisle said loudly. "But first, I'd like everyone in the room to look at this woman. Get a good look at her face."

No one in Lizbeth's field of vision took him up on his offer; they were too busy hiding or crawling away.

"Look at her!" he shouted. "You need to witness this!"

She saw a few heads slowly lift above the tops of their seats, brave souls or foolhardy.

"Get this on the monitor!" Agent Carlisle shouted. "I want her *face* on the goddamned monitor!"

"Don't do it, Carlisle," General Hawthorne said.

Lizbeth thought the general was telling him not to shoot her, like he knew something she didn't since he could see Agent Carlisle's face. Maybe something told him the unbalanced agent was about to pull the trigger. She braced herself, still looking into Zach's eyes. He had moved into a crouch on his chair, lips parted in a snarl. She could tell he wanted to leap across the seat and rip Carlisle's throat out, but the gun wavering only inches from her temple stopped him.

Beyond Zach's head, she saw her frightened face – Caitlin's face – appear on the main monitor.

145

"If she is who she says she is," Agent Carlisle said, "my little demonstration won't work, and I'll let her go."

In the brief moment before she felt him place his hat on her head, she realized what he meant, and what General Hawthorne didn't want him to do. As the iron-laced hat settled down over Caitlin's curls, the pain struck. It was instantaneous and excruciating, lancing through her skull like a spear. She fought to hold her shift, struggling to keep Caitlin's face, but couldn't. All around her, she heard gasps and exclamations as she was forced into her own shape, but all she wanted to do was scream in agony.

"You're hurting her!" Tainie cried. "Please stop!"

"See that?" Agent Carlisle crowed. "This person is not *human*! Neither is that one," he pointed his gun at Tainie, who cringed away in her seat, "or that one," he swung the gun around to Seamus. He was about to point the gun at Zach, too, but the instant the barrel was no longer aimed at Seamus, Zach launched himself out of his seat. Lizbeth was too wrapped up in the pain to see exactly what happened. The gun went off, there was shouting and screaming and then the pain abruptly stopped. Tainie had grabbed the brim of the hat and flung it away.

Zach and Agent Carlisle were locked in hand-to-hand combat, but the struggle didn't last because the soldiers jumped into the fray. Tainie pulled Lizbeth out of her seat and they scrambled into the main aisle as the soldiers separated the combatants. General Hawthorne helped Lizbeth and Tainie to their feet.

"You all right?" he asked.

"Yes," Lizbeth responded. But she wasn't. Just the memory of the pain brought tears to her eyes.

The general gave her a vague pat on the shoulder and nodded to the two soldiers restraining Agent Carlisle. They began to haul him away, but he wasn't going quietly.

"You think you can just toss me aside and no one will ask about what everyone just saw? Those people are aliens! *Aliens*! They nearly destroyed the planet with the Cataclysm and now their people are coming to take over!"

Lizbeth was furious. She wished she had the power to fling fireballs at Agent Carlisle's head, but the only weapon she had was the truth. "We are *not* aliens! We're just as human as you are, except I'm not so sure about you – you monster! We didn't set off the Cataclysm, we stopped it! We saved the planet!" She burst into tears.

"That's a bloody lie!" Agent Carlisle began, but General Hawthorne barked, "Shut him up!" and one of the soldiers punched the agent on the chin. They dragged him away, dazed but still struggling.

The other two soldiers were still restraining Zach, who jerked his arms in an attempt to get loose. General Hawthorne said, "Let him go."

Lizbeth held her arms out and Zach rushed to her. He pulled her tightly to his chest and she buried her face in his shoulder.

Now that the immediate threat had been neutralized, some of the people in the auditorium moved towards the exits, but the majority milled about uneasily, staring in their direction. A group of men from the front row approached the general. Lizbeth was pretty sure they were members of the UN Security Council. One of them, a distinguished gentleman in a grey suit, said, "That man was right. We can't just ignore what we saw."

He turned to Lizbeth and Zach. "What *are* you?"

Chapter Thirty-six

London, England

Zach wasn't about to try to explain what they were – in point of fact, *he* wasn't anything, just a guy with potential. Seamus the Bard, however, was uniquely qualified to take on the task. Zach put a hand on Seamus' back. "You're up, dude."

The man in the grey suit frowned down at the frail old man. "Aren't you H.Q. Spencer?"

"Yes. Yes I am. Storyteller extraordinaire." Seamus spread his hands, in his element. "If I might address the assemblage?" He gestured towards the main floor and the microphone.

General Hawthorne had a deep crease of concern between his eyes, but he allowed Seamus to take center stage.

"Good morning," Seamus began. "I am Harcourt Quincy Spencer. Many of you have grown up reading my novels, and perhaps because of that familiarity, you will trust what I have to say now. I hope so, because it appears that after a very long lifetime of hiding who I really am, it's time to come out of the shadows.

"It's impossible to tell a story that hasn't already been told in one form or another. And in fact, all stories contain a grain of truth, even the most fantastical ones. You think dragons aren't real? They *were* real; we call them dinosaurs now. Imagine what men of old thought upon first encountering the huge fossils of such a beast. Without the benefit of scientific knowledge, they had to come to their own conclusions, and dragons were born.

"I'm using the dragon analogy to illustrate the fact that there are other stories, fairy tales if you will, that have a basis in truth. Despite advances in science which train our brains to disbelieve, legends persist in our hearts.

"Up until recently, I believed in magic. I believed because science had no explanation for the things I knew to be true. You see, shapeshifters exist. They are not born that way; they start out just as human as you are, but there is a substance on Earth – that didn't come from Earth – that can change them.

"That substance was sent to our planet sixty-five million years ago in the form of a comet. It struck Earth and caused global destruction – the extinction event that killed the dinosaurs and, one might say, created dragons."

Seamus laughed a little, but when Zach looked around at the audience, none of them were smiling.

Seamus cleared his throat and continued. "The leader of my people spent her life learning everything she could about the substance and its effect on those who encountered it. By the time the Cataclysm began, she had a working theory that was more far-fetched than any fairy tale, and would probably give even a modern-day science fiction story a run for its money.

"But here we are, confronted by the fact that a spaceship has appeared in our solar system. I ask you to keep that truth in mind when you hear her theory: that our planet's magnetic field had been deliberately converted into a communications satellite for a distant alien race. The comet that the aliens sent was composed of a substance, a biometal that sank into the earth's lithosphere and created a grid – we call it the Gossamer Sphere. They used the sphere for eons, but as humanity spread across the globe and technology advanced, we slowly altered the earth's magnetic field. This interfered with the sphere, muddled their communications, and the Cataclysm occurred because they were attempting to fix it."

There were murmurs throughout the audience, but they died down quickly. Seamus' words had them enthralled. Someone several seats down was filming it all on his cell phone.

"It wasn't until my people came together and contacted the aliens through the sphere that the Cataclysm ended. That is why it stopped so abruptly, because the aliens had no idea we existed – they simply hadn't known we were here. And that is also why I urge you not to jump to conclusions about why they have come. As soon as they learned of us, they shut the Gossamer Sphere down. Those are not the actions of an aggressive race.

"Are there any questions?" He said it with a twist of his lips, like he expected an avalanche of them.

149

Dozens of arms shot up into the air, but one man shouted, "Are *you* a shapeshifter?"

Seamus dipped his head. "Yes."

"Show us!" Someone else called.

Seamus sighed, but complied, shifting into his own face and form, except with two arms. The reaction was a slightly more subdued version of what happened when the radar image of the spaceship appeared on the monitor. General Hawthorne stepped forward, clearly prepared to commandeer the microphone again, but Seamus lifted his hands high above his head and then lowered them slowly, like a conductor. The audience went silent.

"I am neither magical creature nor alien. I am human, like you. Every one of you has the potential deep within you to become like me. When the comet struck Earth, microscopic particles of the biometal permeated the atmosphere, the water, and every surface on the planet. The DNA of the animals that survived was altered by it. Our leader believes that shapeshifting characteristics are coded in everyone's DNA, but a catalyst must be introduced. Just like radiation or toxins can result in cancer, if a person today were exposed to the biometal it would either kill them or change them."

There were more questions, of course. Zach, Lizbeth and Tainie sat back in their seats and listened as Seamus expertly fielded them. Zach had to admit Seamus was good – truly a master at controlling his audience.

If anyone could get them out of this alive, it was Seamus and his silver tongue.

Chapter Thirty-seven

London, England

The misty remnants of the storm had dissipated by the time Bill drove through the outskirts of London, giving Kevin an unobstructed view of the city streets and the people on them. He observed the exact same kind of behavior he'd seen during the Cataclysm. The highway leaving the city was gridlocked. A car was on fire on one street and looting was in progress on another. It seemed as if some people, at least, hadn't learned any lessons from the Cataclysm. Panic was the order of the day.

"I don't understand why they're freaking out so badly," Kevin said. "They don't even know whether the aliens are hostile."

Bill flipped the turn signal and pulled into a petrol station. The lines for the pumps were already four and five cars deep, and he got into the shortest of them. "But they *could* be hostile. It's the possibility that's frightening."

Tara reached into the neck of her shirt and pulled out a small gold cross on a chain. "I'll bet there are a lot of religious folks out there questionin' their beliefs right about now."

Kevin tilted his head to look at the necklace and she said, "I'm not one them, in case you're wonderin'. This was my grandmother's."

"And don't forget, Kevin, how you felt when you first learned things in the world weren't as you'd supposed," Caitlin said. "There will be an adjustment period, and some will handle it better than others."

"Yeah, I guess," he said. "But why do they have to destroy things and hurt each other? It's embarrassing. The aliens are going to think we're a bunch of savages."

"I suspect we are, compared to them," Caitlin said. "Let's hope they understand that."

Tara said she needed to use the loo, so Kevin escorted her inside the station's convenience store. The man behind the register had a shotgun resting on the counter. When Tara asked for the key to the bathroom, he said, "Only for customers."

"We're getting gas," Kevin said, but the man gave him such a dark look he grabbed a package of donuts and said, "I'll take these."

By the time they got back into the car, Bill was pumping gas and Caitlin was staring out the window pensively.

"Where are we going, anyway?" Kevin asked.

"Bill says they took Lizbeth to a military command center," Caitlin said. "I have a few ideas where it might be, but the trick will be verifying she's inside."

Bill opened the door and got into the driver's seat. Before he shut it, Kevin heard the nearby cawing of a raven. He looked out the window and saw a large black bird with distinctively blue eyes sitting on top of the fuel dispenser.

"Caw?" he said with an amazed laugh. He pulled the window switch and as soon as the top of the glass came even with the door frame, the bird flew down and landed on it.

"Whoa." Tara leaned back in her seat. "That's odd."

"Not odd," Caitlin said. "Fortuitous. Caw is Zach's bird. Last I heard, Caw was with him in the states. I don't believe a raven capable of flying across the Atlantic, so there's only one reason I can think of that would explain his presence. Zach is here."

"Who's Zach? And how did his bird find us?" Tara asked.

Kevin laughed again, looking fondly at Caw. "Zach's one of us. I heard a raven's cry at Simon's house. What do you want to bet he followed us from there?"

Caw jumped onto his shoulder and rubbed his head against Kevin's chin before leaning down and pecking at the paper bag holding the doughnuts. Kevin opened the box and broke off a piece for the bird, who jabbed at it with his beak.

"Maybe he can lead us to Zach," he said.

The car behind them beeped its horn, so Bill shifted into drive and pulled away from the pumps. "Well, I suppose I could follow him if you can get him to show me the way."

Kevin rolled up the window as Caw gobbled down the piece of doughnut. "I'm not sure how."

"Just ask him," Tara said, leaning down and looking into one of Caw's eyes. "Where's Zach, birdie?"

152

"He's special, but he doesn't understand English," Kevin said. But Caw *had* apparently understood Kevin once, the time the bird allowed Kevin to put him in Zach's backpack. Kevin had mimicked some of the sounds Caw made, but even then hadn't really believed it was the sounds that got the bird to cooperate.

He looked into Caw's eye, just as Tara had, but instead of verbalizing his request, he visualized it: a memory of Zach's face. Caw ruffled his feathers and uttered a sandpapery little squawk, but otherwise did nothing.

"Maybe if we showed him a map," Bill suggested. "Like Google satellite. Something he might recognize from above."

"I wonder." Caitlin leaned her elbow on the center console's armrest and held her chin in her hand. They were driving north on a main thoroughfare. She looked out the front windshield and then back at the bird. "Take the next right turn."

Bill shrugged and turned on his blinker. He wasn't even halfway through the turn when Caw let out several distressed squawks and began flapping his wings, claws scratching at the doorframe.

"Okay, okay, I get it," Kevin said. He rolled the window back down and Caw flew out.

Bill pulled over and they watched as Caw circled the intersection they'd just left and then landed on a light pole.

Bill did an illegal u-turn and drove back. As soon as they got within twenty or so yards of him, the raven took off again, flying above the thoroughfare.

"It sure looks like he's leading us somewhere," Bill said.

They followed Caw for almost an hour, long enough for Kevin to begin seriously doubting whether they should have put their faith in the bird. The only thing that gave him hope was the fact that Caw hadn't led them in circles or zigzags. On the contrary, they'd kept a steady northerly course.

The bird took them through a sparsely populated area and then down a secluded road with one sign that read "No Through Road" and another that read, "Private Property. No Trespassing." The last building they'd passed was about a kilometer behind them when Tara asked, "What's that?" She pointed up ahead, past dozens of cars and vans parked along the shoulder.

A high chain link fence with barbed wire strung along the top stretched across the road. On the inside, patrolling the barrier, were armed soldiers. At least thirty people milled about outside the fence. Among the vehicles on the side of the road were several news vans, and some of the people in the crowd carried professional video equipment or held microphones.

Bill pulled over and parked behind the last car. Up ahead, Caw had landed in a tree on the other side of the fence.

"I believe we've arrived," Caitlin said.

Chapter Thirty-eight

London, England

Lizbeth noticed Seamus said nothing to the crowd about exactly how old he was, or about his mind-reading abilities. She could hardly imagine how he'd break something like *that* to them. No matter how carefully he phrased it, there was really no tactful way to say, "Oh, and by the way, not only can I pose as any one of you whenever I choose, but I can intrude upon your very thoughts."

It wouldn't go over well with anyone, but especially not this crowd. She'd assessed them as a whole based on the questions they asked and their reactions to the answers, and found them intelligent and mostly open-minded, but the latter might have more to do with the setting. They fed off each other's emotions in a dynamic kind of way that Seamus seemed to have tapped into. It could have turned into a mob mentality, but whenever someone attempted to emphasize a negative, he deftly turned it around. Once these powerful men and women were back at the helm of whatever agency they ran, however, Lizbeth suspected their doubts would reassert themselves – especially when they tried to explain things to the people they answered to.

With any luck, she'd be far from the spotlight by then...and not at the bottom of some deep, dark jail cell.

Seamus had just answered the same question for the third or fourth time, hopefully an indication that the interrogation would end soon. Lizbeth was starving and really needed to use the restroom, plus, even though it wasn't high on her list of priorities, she was self-conscious that she'd been wearing the same clothes for over twenty-four hours. Zach had been tenderly holding her hand since Seamus had begun talking. If he noticed how grungy she was, he didn't let on.

"What was the deal with that hat?" he asked.

After she told him how the hat forced her to shift because it was lined with iron, he kissed her hand and said, "It hurt?"

She fought back a resurgence of tears. "A *lot*."

"Poor baby," he murmured, and then added, "And poor Seamus. Clapped in irons for fourteen years."

She was about to ask him to explain, but a disturbance on the other side of the center circle caught her attention. The NASA lady, Stella something, was waving her arms, trying to get General Hawthorne's attention. She didn't try very long before jumping up and running over to him. Whatever she said made his mouth drop open. A quickly controlled look of dismay crossed his face.

He strode up to Seamus and took the microphone. Calmly but firmly, he said, "Ladies and gentlemen, I'm going to have to summarily end this meeting. Each of you will want to make immediate arrangements to return to your home offices. It appears the ships are on the move – NASA estimates they will arrive in near space within the next two to three hours."

Pandemonium struck again. This time there was pushing and shoving as everyone attempted to exit the building at once. General Hawthorne hovered next to Seamus, whether to protect him or to ensure he didn't try to escape, Lizbeth couldn't say.

She, Zach and Tainie moved to stand in the aisle, waiting for General Hawthorne to let them know what was in store for them. The remaining two soldiers kept anyone from getting near. Several people, in groups or alone, stopped to talk to General Hawthorne briefly before leaving. In a surprisingly short amount of time, the auditorium was nearly empty, and the video conference monitors had gone black, all but the central one, which still had the image of the spaceship on it.

The general took a phone call, so Seamus started towards them, but he'd only take a few steps when a group of five men came in the main entrance. They headed straight for the general, who held up a hand to stave them off while he continued his call. Lizbeth recognized Agent Collins from this morning and exchanged a concerned look with Tainie. The other men with Collins were strangers, but they were all wearing knapsacks over their shoulders and had those horrible black hats on their heads. It struck her that the bad guys always wore black hats.

Agent Collins didn't wait for the general to finish his call. He slapped a sheaf of papers against the general's chest and his raised voice carried in the auditorium. "...orders signed by the Chief of the Defense Staff himself!"

"Who are they?" Zach asked. It took her a second to realize he'd spoken to the soldier standing next to him, a thick-necked young man with a doughy nose.

It seemed at first as if the soldier wasn't going to answer, but he finally said in a heavy Scottish brogue, "That would be Secret Intelligence Service." The muscles in his jaw worked briefly, then he surprised her by addressing her directly, "Can I really be like you?"

It wasn't exactly an offer of friendship, but it was the first chink in the armor of any of the soldiers guarding them, and she didn't want to blow it by discouraging him. She forced a smile. "I was lucky it didn't kill me. You'd be taking a huge chance if you tried."

"It'd be worth it," the soldier replied, looking back towards the men confronting the general. His hand had unconsciously strayed to rest on his weapon.

"*Lizbeth.*" She heard it in her head and shifted her gaze to Seamus, who was standing beside a very angry looking General Hawthorne. "*These men say they're authorized to take us from the general's custody. I suspect the changing of the guard will not benefit us.*"

Lizbeth didn't suspect it, she knew. General Hawthorne had been open and honest with her, while Carlisle and Collins had treated them like animals. Why the general seemed to have gone out of his way to protect them, she couldn't say, but it looked as if his influence had reached its limit.

She caught some of what he was saying, "...not going anywhere until I verify...supposed to be working together on this."

"The bloody alien ships are on their way!" Agent Collins practically shouted. His face was red with fury. "*Your* job is to protect this country from invaders. *Our* job is military intelligence. These creatures are *our* purview, not yours!"

"Creatures...?" Tainie murmured. "Is that how they see us?"

"Fear will do that to a person," Zach replied.

General Hawthorne started to say something, but Agent Collins was so worked up, he interrupted him. "We know about your family, know you think you have something in common with these mutants, but they won't give you quarter if it comes to that. You're just as expendable as the rest of us. They've been replacing kings and queens for centuries, changing history to suit themselves. And now they've sent for their people."

Seamus laughed derisively. "That's Guild rhetoric. You've just given away your agenda."

Agent Collins turned on Seamus, snapping, "We've always had one agenda: to protect the human race from filth like you."

Lizbeth recoiled as the agent made a hocking sound and spat in Seamus' face. He then gave a hand signal that had the other four agents suddenly pulling their guns and advancing on Lizbeth's group. The Scottish soldier who'd spoken to her started to draw his weapon, but the closest agent called out, "Easy does it. We're authorized to take custody of the subjects. You Toms best not make this harder than need be."

The soldiers reluctantly lifted their hands.

Lizbeth looked at Seamus. In her head, he said, *"They're Guild. Escape if you can. This may be your last chance."*

Next to her, Tainie's indrawn breath told her she'd heard him, too.

"Zach," Lizbeth whispered shakily. "Seamus says they're Guild. Get us out of this."

A sound from the back of the auditorium made everyone turn. The two soldiers who'd been left guarding the side door had come in, rifles at the ready.

Lizbeth barely had time to register the danger of being caught in the crossfire when Zach yelled, "Get down!" He shoved her ahead of him, between the nearest rows of seats. Tainie had hunched down at the same moment, so they were somewhat protected when the gun battle began.

Chapter Thirty-nine

London, England

Zach pushed Lizbeth and said, "Go! Go! *Go!*" She began to crawl rapidly towards the next aisle. Shouts and cracking gunfire echoed through the auditorium. A glance around told him the four agents were no longer in sight – they'd either gotten shot or, more likely, had scattered and were hidden among the seats like the rest of them. The auditorium was softly lit and provided perfect cover.

The two soldiers who'd come in the back way had split up and were running stooped over along the back wall. The Scottish soldier was out of sight, but Zach got a quick glimpse of Seamus and General Hawthorne struggling with Agent Collins before the other soldier dropped to a crouch in the aisle and blocked his view.

Zach started to follow Lizbeth, but as he turned an agent popped up and took a shot at them. The soldier took it in the chest. He was wearing a vest, but the shooter's gun had a heavy kick to it, enough to knock him off his feet and put him flat on his back, gasping for breath. Zach grabbed his arm and hauled his upper body behind the seats.

"Gimme your gun," Zach said. "I'm a cop."

Through the pain, the soldier looked at him like he was out of his mind. Zach figured that would be his reaction, but thought he'd try the polite way first. The impolite way, forcing the downed man to release the pistol, was his next move. He was about to drop his knee onto the soldier's forearm, but a bullet came right through the seat behind him and grazed his shoulder. He threw himself flat to the ground.

From this vantage point, he saw the lower half of the shooter through the seat legs. The soldier saw him, too, and lifted his gun unsteadily.

"Dude, let me," Zach whispered.

The soldier hesitated then handed the gun over, muttering, "Dinna make me regret it."

Zach hefted the pistol and took aim. The shooter was squatting, and the cuffs of his pants had risen to reveal black leather oxfords with black socks. Zach didn't want to kill him if he didn't have to, so instead of shooting him in the thigh where he might hit an artery, he targeted the man's ankle and squeezed off a round. The shooter let out a yell of pain and fell backward, dropping his gun. Zach quickly aimed for the gun and shot it out of the fallen agent's reach. "One down, four to go."

"You're bleedin'," the soldier said.

Zach glanced down at his shoulder. "It's a scratch." He held the pistol out, but the soldier made a face and said, "Keep it. Go protect your girlfriend."

Another series of shots rang out and someone yelled, "Don't shoot!" It was hard to tell where it came from with the acoustics in the auditorium, but he thought it originated from behind and to the left of his position. He'd lost sight of Lizbeth, who'd crawled far enough away that the curve of the row concealed her. There was no sign of Seamus and the general, or Collins.

Zach helped the soldier to a sitting position and waited for him to unsling the rifle from his shoulder. Once he was in position, Zach said, "Cover me." Bent nearly double, he ran along the row in Lizbeth's direction. Someone cracked off two shots in rapid succession and the upholstery of the seat to the right of him exploded. A third shot came from behind and someone grunted in pain; the soldier had nailed the shooter. Zach kept running, but then tripped over something and fell. At first, he thought he'd tromped all over Lizbeth, but when he reached out all he encountered was a pile of clothing.

Oh, no, he thought, a chill of fear sweeping over him. He looked through the seat legs in all directions but didn't see anything but another pile of clothes. She and Tainie would have chosen something stealthy, something fast and deadly – but no matter how smart her choice, there was no animal on Earth impervious to bullets.

Chapter Forty

London, England

Kevin and the others lurked on the fringes of the crowd, eavesdropping to try to determine what was happening here. On the far side of the chain link fence, some distance down the road, a row of wide evergreen trees partially shielded a two-story brick building from prying eyes. Presumably, it was the military command center Bill told Caitlin about.

A stretch limousine, of all things, drove up the road toward the fence. The driver signaled to one of the soldiers to let them out, but the throng of reporters gathered in the street made it impossible. Cameras rolled and flashbulbs burst even though the occupants of the car were anonymous behind tinted windows.

Kevin happened to be standing close enough to the fence to hear the nearest soldier call for backup on his radio. Within a short amount of time, several armed vehicles arrived. Soldiers poured out and the reporters reluctantly backed off enough to allow the gates to be opened. After that, more cars arrived, dozens of them. As they began streaming out, the soldiers were forced to create a blockade along either side of the road with their bodies. The occupants of the cars ignored the frantically shouted questions of the reporters.

It was the questions that told Kevin what had gone on in the building.

"Was the meeting a success? What decisions were made?"

"Exactly how long until the spaceships arrive?"

"Will we be launching an offensive?"

"How many shapeshifters are in custody?"

"Is it true H.Q. Spencer is an alien?"

The H.Q. Spencer reference stumped him, but the gist of it was that a meeting had been held and certain secrets revealed. Had they tortured it out of Lizbeth? And why was Zach here?

Nearby, a cameraman was recording a woman reporter. She straightened her jacket, licked her lips and at a signal from the cameraman, began talking.

"The cars you see behind me are leaving a clandestine early morning meeting of some of the world's most influential leaders and heads of state. Preliminary reports tell us the meeting broke up suddenly because the latest radar images from NASA indicate the objects they've identified, presumably alien spaceships, will arrive within the next few hours. We've obtained exclusive unretouched video from within the meeting offering proof that the aliens are living amongst us and have been for some time. The facts have not been substantiated, but – oh, I'm told we're going to show the clip..."

Kevin turned to Caitlin. "They think we're...?"

"Of course they do. It's the logical conclusion." She glanced in the direction of the brick building. "We need to get them out of there."

The line of cars had trickled down to a few coming up the road now and then. Some of the reporters were packing up and leaving as well, but most stayed. Kevin suspected they were hoping to get a glimpse of the 'aliens' inside the building.

One of the soldiers was staring at Bill with a frown between his brows. He walked over, one hand resting casually on the rifle slung over his shoulder.

"I saw them detain you back at the facility," he said. "What are you doing here?"

Caitlin responded before Bill could. "We need to speak with General Hawthorne. It's quite urgent."

The soldier opened his mouth to reply, but a burst of static came from the tactical radio at his belt, followed by a man shouting, "Shots fired!" and something else Kevin couldn't make out. The soldier must have understood it, however, because he lifted the radio to his mouth and said, "Copy that."

He whirled around and broke into a trot, waving to his companions. "Move out! Let's go!"

"Did he say shots fired?" Tara asked.

"He did," Caitlin replied. She started walking along the fence, away from the road. Kevin and the others hurried to keep up. After about a hundred yards, she veered away from the fence and approached the trees.

The vegetation near the fence had been cleared so nothing grew high enough to provide a way over, but the trees were old growth, stretching far above them. She stepped around the nearest one, a big evergreen, and began to undress.

Kevin turned his back to give her privacy and caught a look of confusion on Tara's face. "What's she doin'?" she whispered.

"She's going to shift into something that doesn't wear clothes," he replied.

Bill spoke softly, but his voice carried. "I don't suppose I can talk you out of this."

"We'll need a getaway driver," Caitlin replied. "Can I count on you?"

His short laugh was self-derogatory. "Sure, why not? You know I'd do anything for you."

Kevin expected Caitlin to give him a hard time about that claim, but all she said was, "Thank you."

The next sound Kevin heard was a rough scratching. He looked around and saw Caitlin climbing the tree as a white jaguar, her signature shift. When she got high enough, she shifted again, into a very large white seabird – an albatross, he thought. She launched from the tree in the opposite direction from the building, probably to avoid the attention of the soldiers. She would gain altitude and fly straight down over the building rather than giving anyone a target.

"Why don't you go with her?" Tara asked.

"I can't fly," Kevin said. He unzipped his jacket, though, and shrugged out of it.

"Why not? If you become a bird, isn't it instinctive?"

"Not really. Not for me."

Tara shaded her eyes with her hand and watched Caitlin until she was a speck in the sky. "What are we going to do?"

Kevin pulled his shirt off. "*You* are going to wait here with Bill."

"I want to help."

"And I want you safe. They have guns, Tara."

Her bottom lip protruded a bit, reminding him how young she was and how sheltered she'd been. "Fine," she said. "I won't follow you. I'm sure I'd just be a liability."

He took her hand and squeezed it, lingering only a moment before letting go.

After stripping off the rest of his clothes, self-conscious even though no one was looking, he shifted. It was cold out; not ideal weather for a

163

python, but he wanted to get to the fence unseen. He slithered through the grass, aware of Tara's gasp of surprise as she spied him, but his brain was strangely sluggish in this form and he struggled to stay focused on the goal. When he got to the fence, he followed it for about a hundred yards looking for an opening wide enough to get his body through but didn't find one.

He shifted again, into an aardvark this time. He sealed off his nostrils from the dust and began to dig, quickly making a hole under the fence big enough for his python body. After shifting back into the python, he slid through the hole.

All of the reporters were gone. The original two soldiers had stayed to guard the main gate and hadn't noticed him, but at the rate he was going, it would take forever to get to the main building. He needed to choose an animal that was so fast it wouldn't matter if he didn't make it undetected. He decided on a cheetah and began to run as soon as he'd shifted. His semi-retractable claws dug into the ground as his long legs made short work of the distance to the parking lot. The vehicles that had been at the gate were just pulling up to the building, soldiers jumping out. They split into groups and began to surround the structure.

Kevin ran across a section of the parking lot, claws scraping the tarmac. He stopped briefly next to a car before shooting past two armored vehicles. He heard a shout from behind, but kept running, his goal a cluster of giant arborvitae growing against one of the building's walls. As soon as he made the safety of the tall bushes, he shifted again, back into the chimpanzee form he'd found so useful at the grove.

The building was two stories tall at its center, but this section of wall was only one story. He climbed the arborvitae, making it to the roof easily. He lay flat on the graveled tarpaper and looked over the edge, spotting two soldiers by one of the armored vehicles. One of the soldiers was gesturing in his direction, clearly telling the other what he'd seen. With his attention directed at the soldiers, Kevin was taken by surprise when Caitlin glided down and landed at his feet.

She didn't chastise him for being there, just tilted her head towards the wall of the second story and sent, *"Try the door."*

Chapter Forty-one

London, England

The seats in the auditorium were upholstered in burgundy fabric and the navy-blue carpet was patterned with burgundy and black swirls. Lizbeth's fur was dark orangey brown with black spots. She felt under the circumstances that she blended in quite well, especially since she kept to the shadows, weaving in and out of the seat legs.

Tainie stayed close as they made their way to the main exit. Lizbeth didn't know what they were going to do once they got there, but the whole shift-into-a-leopard thing had been an impromptu plan concocted as a last resort.

She'd never been a leopard before, but knew big cats were one of Caitlin's favorite shifts. After only a few minutes slinking silently through the auditorium, she thought she knew why. For one thing, her vision had significantly improved. She'd already spotted one soldier along the back wall behind a trash receptacle and an agent hidden among the seats, and could hear a third man breathing heavily somewhere nearby. All were easy to avoid. As she and Tainie circumnavigated the heavily breathing agent, the sharp scent of blood assaulted her senses. Her empty stomach cramped up and her mouth began to water. She had to fight the urge to investigate.

When they reached the last row on the edge of the main aisle, they looked out across what seemed an insurmountably vast space between them and the glass doors leading to the lobby. The lights in the auditorium were low to begin with, and someone had shut them off entirely in the lobby, so it was black beyond the doors.

"*Should we run for it?*" Tainie sent.

"*Or maybe try to sneak along the wall?*" Lizbeth suggested, although neither option appealed to her.

"*How do we open the doors? We've got paws.*"

"*Good question. We could change back to ourselves when we get there.*"

"*Yeah, but we'd be naked.*"

"*True.*" Lizbeth sat on her haunches and her ears perked up at a noise out in the lobby. "*Hear that?*"

"*Sounds like footsteps...lots of them.*"

"*There were tons of soldiers out there. I bet they've got all the exits blocked.*"

"*Is that good or bad?*" Tainie asked.

Lizbeth looked over her shoulder at Tainie, whose fur was slightly darker. "*Bad. They'll probably shoot first and ask questions later.*"

"*Or...*" Tainie blinked guileless yellow eyes. "*Considering we'll be naked, they'll be too busy staring to consider us a threat...*"

There was nothing funny about their situation, but Lizbeth found herself laughing anyway, and it came out like a squeaky purr.

She heard more footsteps, this time from within the auditorium. She hugged the ground and eased backward as the soldier behind the trash can ran right up to the chair she was hiding under. He smelled of sweat and something else, something unpleasantly pungent.

If fear had a scent, it would smell like that, she thought.

It wasn't until Tainie sent, "*Yeah, really,*" that she realized she'd projected the thought.

She could only see the soldier's lower half, but he held a tactical radio in his left hand. He lifted it and whispered, "I'm in position." Lizbeth heard a thin response over the radio, "Roger that. Any sign of the boss?"

"Negative."

"Initiating plan alpha."

Lizbeth wished she could see into the soldier's eyes to find out what plan alpha was, but the main doors suddenly burst open and the barrels of several rifles appeared from the gloom. A man with a bullhorn announced, "The building is surrounded. Give yourselves up and you will be treated fairly."

Plan alpha wasn't much of a plan as far as Lizbeth was concerned; it was more like the direct approach. She assumed the man with the bullhorn was talking to the MI6 agents and not the rest of them, but if he was talking to her, she wasn't budging. She had a feeling the agents wouldn't give up so easily either, but to her surprise, someone yelled, "Don't shoot!"

Arms lifted from among the seats and Agent Collins slowly stood.

Tainie growled a little in her throat.

"I'm unarmed," Collins shouted.

166

"*Lizbeth,*" Tainie sent. "*Agent Collins was my English teacher and I'd know his voice anywhere. That's not it.*"

Now wasn't the time to ask Tainie to expound upon that bizarre statement. If it wasn't Collins, then it could only be Seamus standing there unarmed in a room full of agents who wanted to kill him.

Chapter Forty-two

London, England

Not only did Zach recognize Seamus' voice, but 'Collins' was wearing H.Q. Spencer's buttoned up sweater with the patches on the elbows. What was Seamus *doing*?

After a tense couple of seconds, someone on the other side of the auditorium shouted, "Don't fall for it! That's not me!"

As the rifles at the lobby doors swung in the direction of Collins' voice, Seamus ducked back down behind the seats and Zach understood. Seamus had made a target of himself to locate Collins for the soldiers and prevent this confrontation from escalating into a conflict that would potentially kill them all. It was a selfless, reckless act of bravery, and Zach felt the last of his resentment towards the shapeshifter melt away.

Collins was Guild, which made the man a fanatic, but he'd been smart enough to resist taking a shot at Seamus just now, smart enough to know it would have resulted in swift retaliation. Was that an indication he wasn't willing to sacrifice himself for his beliefs? Zach had a bad feeling what it really meant was that Collins felt he had other options.

The man with the bullhorn said, "I am Lieutenant Colonel Sheldon Paxton. I've been in contact with General Hawthorne via his cell phone and he would like to negotiate the terms of your surrender. We're on a bit of a timetable, as I'm sure you are aware."

"My terms," Collins shouted, "are the same as they ever were! Give us the shapeshifters before they succeed in destroying the planet!"

Paxton quickly responded. "I'm told you and Agent Carlisle are members of a sleeper cell for an organization dedicated to destroying the shapeshifters. Do your men realize this? Do they know you aren't acting as a representative of the MI6 in this regard?"

They do now, Zach thought, hoping the knowledge would make a difference in how the agents reacted.

Collins decided at that point to stand. He held his hands out – one was empty, but the other clutched something small, like a cell phone. He was several rows back and over from where Seamus had been, and something about the look on his face made Zach very uneasy.

"Doesn't matter what they think!" Collins said. "They follow orders. You'd best tell your men to back off. This theatre has been seeded with enough explosives to wipe out everyone here!"

Zach was just itching to shoot the jerk, but he noticed Collins held the item in his hand with his thumb up, suggestive of a trigger device. If it *was* a trigger, and Zach shot him, the whole place could blow. The knapsacks the agents had been carrying were probably how they got the explosives into the auditorium. Zach wished he could read Collins' mind, but according to Lizbeth, even Seamus wouldn't be able to read him as long as he had that hat on his head.

He hoped Lizbeth had gotten out. He looked around, trying to locate the exits – the obvious ones like the doors, and the ones a shapeshifter could potentially use. There were plenty of air vents, but the ones he could see were too far up the wall for her to access. His gaze skimmed across a long, narrow window high up at the back of the auditorium and then jerked back as he caught a movement behind the glass.

It was the projection booth, and someone was in the room looking down on the drama below.

Chapter Forty-three

London, England

The door on the roof of the building had been locked, but there were two windows to the left of it. They weren't the kind that opened, but they weren't made from reinforced glass either. Kevin got the impression the building hadn't originally been a 'military command center.' The Cataclysm had caused so much destruction, many structures had been repurposed. From the cigarette butts littering the rooftop, it appeared someone liked to come out here on their breaks. A brick near the door indicated they had to prop it open, probably to keep it from automatically locking. The brick made short work of one of the windows and Kevin and Caitlin, in the form of chimpanzees, climbed over the sill and entered an office.

From the office, they went out into a dark hallway with a door on one side and a set of stairs on the other. They descended the stairs and Kevin cautiously cracked the door at the bottom to look out. It was the building's lobby and appeared to be filled with soldiers. Just as he gently closed the door, someone on a bullhorn said, "The building is surrounded. Give yourselves up and you will be treated fairly."

At first, he thought the warning was for them, but then someone shouted something he couldn't make out. He started back up the stairs, but Caitlin put a hand on his arm and shifted into the white jaguar. Her ears perked up and she turned her head to get a bead on whatever was being said.

"*I can hear them, but I'm not sure what's going on,*" she sent.

After the man with the bullhorn announced he wanted to negotiate the terms of someone's surrender, Caitlin slipped past Kevin and began climbing the stairs.

"*It's not directed at us,*" she sent, but then stopped in her tracks when the man with the bullhorn talked about a sleeper cell that wanted to destroy shapeshifters. Kevin could hear a man shouting his response, but still couldn't make out the words.

Caitlin could, however. She turned wide yellow eyes on him before running up the staircase. He followed, partially swinging his way along the stair rails to keep up.

Retracing their steps, they went past the office and tried the door on the far side. It was a projection booth, but from the boxes and junk stored in the small room, it was obviously in disuse. A long, narrow window looked out over an auditorium, and as it happened, that was where all the action appeared to be.

He saw several men scattered here and there, all but one crouched down among the sea of chairs.

"*I know him,*" Caitlin sent. "*His name is Collins. He must be Guild. They've infiltrated MI6.*"

"*I don't see Lizbeth, but I think that's Zach.*" Kevin pointed.

"*She's down there, and Tainie, and...Seamus, I believe. Collins claims to have planted explosives in the auditorium.*"

"*Can you read him? Is he telling the truth?*"

Caitlin made a 'rowr' sound that Kevin interpreted as frustration. "*No,*" she sent. "*They've lined their hats with iron.*"

Kevin didn't ask if she thought this Collins guy was crazy enough to blow himself up along with everyone in the auditorium. He already knew the answer. "*Can you contact Lizbeth?*"

"*Not from here, but I'll try Seamus, he's more adept.*"

After a moment, she sent, "*I can't reach him. Maybe if we get closer.*"

The man on the bullhorn said something again, but Kevin tuned it out. With all the soldiers around, it would be impossible to get closer, but he had an idea.

"*What if instead of getting closer, we got stronger? I could go back, get the kernel out of my pocket.*"

But a noise outside the projection room door dashed that hope. The soldiers were on to them. The one who'd seen a cheetah running across the parking lot and a monkey climbing up to the roof must have convinced the others to investigate.

Kevin reached out and quietly turned the lock on the doorknob. It wouldn't hold them off if they really wanted in, but it might slow them down. He and Caitlin were now effectively boxed in. The window overlooking the auditorium didn't open and even if they smashed it, there was a twenty-foot drop. The door was the only way in or out.

He went to the window and looked out again. Zach's pale face was turned up in their direction. The man Caitlin had referred to as Collins stood there defiantly punching the air with his right hand, which was closed around something. Kevin could see his mouth moving, his face contorted in anger as if he were berating the room at large. Behind him was a wall of monitors, probably the reason the projection booth was no longer in use. The central monitor had an image on it. With a little shock of surprise, he realized it was the spaceship. When he saw the triskele symbol etched into the metal, he leaned his forehead against the glass and stared, dumbfounded.

In his peripheral vision he was vaguely aware of Caitlin studying the ceiling. "*We'll have to try the ventilation system.*"

There was something about the symbol that held his attention, something important, something hovering right at the edge of his consciousness, like it was...a *key* to something.

He held a hand out in Caitlin's direction. "*Wait,*" he sent, struggling against a sudden rush of images and words. He turned and leaned back against the wall, slowly sliding down until he was sitting in a slump.

"*What's wrong?*"

"*I remember now.*"

"*Remember what? Kevin, get up. I need your help.*"

He didn't respond. In his mind, he was back in the cairn with Tara, looking up at the ceiling where the triskele symbol had been carved into the stone lintel long ago. He'd dozed off thinking about the aliens, wondering about them. When he woke, Tara told him he'd been speaking a strange language in his sleep. Caitlin hadn't been there, hadn't been privy to that conversation.

"*I was the one who initiated contact. Both times,*" he sent. "*Not them.*"

Caitlin put a paw on his shoulder as someone rattled the doorknob. "*We'll discuss this later.*"

"*You don't understand. It wasn't the cairn or the oak grove that gave me access to the sphere, it was the triskele symbol. Like the one on the crown.*"

"*That doesn't help our current situation. I need you to focus.*"

He stood, excited now. "*That's just it – focus! All I have to do is think of the symbol and I can use the sphere.*"

"*Use it? How? We can't just call the aliens and ask them to help us. We need to get out of this room now!*"

"*No,*" he sent, turning back to look out the window. "*We need to stop that man from killing our friends.*"

Chapter Forty-four

London, England

Lizbeth listened to Collins spew vile, hateful words against them, worried that he would convince the general to give them up. When the man on the bullhorn, Lieutenant Colonel Paxton, said, "Let's make a deal. You tell us where the explosives are and we'll give you the shapeshifters," she almost freaked out.

Was it another ruse, or had the general decided to cut his losses? Either way, Collins didn't go for it.

"No, you give me the shapeshifters and none of us go boom. In that order. You have three minutes to decide." He tilted his arm and looked at his watch to emphasize his sincerity.

"*We need to make a break for it,*" Tainie sent.

Lizbeth stared past Lieutenant Colonel Paxton's legs into the gloom of the lobby. She knew Tainie was right. Running was their only chance, but it would mean leaving Zach behind. If Collins set the explosives off in response to their escape attempt and killed Zach and Seamus, she'd never forgive herself – assuming she got far enough away to survive the blast.

One thing was for sure, Collins didn't want to die for his beliefs. He would have already done it if that was his intention. She didn't dare hope that he was stalling because there weren't any explosives. She couldn't read his mind, but doubted he'd have such conviction in his voice if he was lying.

Running was the logical thing to do.

"Two minutes!" Collins shouted.

Lizbeth looked at Tainie. "*Are you ready?*"

Tainie nodded.

Lizbeth's lean muscles tensed, but a strange sensation made her hesitate. It was a gentle electric tingling that started at the base of her spine and got stronger as it spread throughout her body. It felt like she'd touched a

173

live wire, reminiscent of what she'd experienced during the Cataclysm each time the gossamer sphere adjusted itself.

"*You feel that?*" she sent.

"*Yeah,*" Tainie responded. "*Reminds me of the Cataclysm. What is it?*"

"*I think it's...the sphere!*" Had the aliens arrived and turned the gossamer sphere back on?

Tainie looked away, severing their mental contact, but she heard, "*Lizbeth, Seamus, Tainie, it's Kevin. Can you hear me?*"

"*Yes! Where are you?*" Lizbeth's internal voice was almost drowned out by Seamus and Tainie as all of them responded at once. It was disorienting to have so many voices in her head at the same time.

In the background, she heard Collins shout, "One minute!"

Lieutenant Colonel Paxton waved to his men and they backed off some. The soldier squatting next to her chair dropped flat and put his arms over his head.

Kevin sent, "*I've activated the sphere. When I say go, I want all of you to run for the door. Do you hear me?*"

Lizbeth had no idea how he had done what he claimed, or how the sphere would help them, but she didn't question it. She simply said, "*Yes.*"

"Ten, nine, eight..." Collins yelled.

She glared at the man, hoping Kevin's plan worked, but then Zach appeared with a gun in his hand, walking jerkily up the main aisle as if he could barely manage it. Had he been shot? His coat was black, so she couldn't see any blood, but there was definitely something wrong with him, and he obviously hadn't heard Kevin, or he wouldn't be confronting Collins now.

"If you shoot me," Collins said, "you'll all die with me."

"Maybe," Zach replied. "Or maybe you're lying and a bullet to the head will shut you up."

Collins lifted his eyebrows and grinned, the defiant response of a cornered man about to do something desperate.

Suddenly Lizbeth felt a powerful surge of energy and in an instant, Collins disappeared from view, a column of silver fire surrounding him.

In her head, she heard the word, "*Run!*"

Tainie shot off in the direction of the lobby, but Lizbeth looked at Zach, who was just standing there staring at the column of energy. He wasn't fae and hadn't heard Kevin the first time, so for sure he hadn't heard Kevin tell them to run.

She darted over to him and nudged his legs, but he didn't respond.

Lieutenant Colonel Paxton must have put two and two together, because he shouted through the bullhorn to his men to evacuate. The soldiers still in the auditorium, and the MI6 agents, too, scrambled to get out.

Zach was still standing there as if he couldn't move. Lizbeth recalled how badly the sphere had affected him during the Cataclysm – of them all, he had been the most sensitive to its power. He wasn't frozen in fear or shock, he was just *frozen*, as if his nervous system was overwhelmed.

Thinking quickly, she shifted into a gorilla and found that despite their difference in size, she was able to easily bend him over her shoulder in a fireman's carry. As she hustled him into the lobby, Seamus appeared at her side, carrying the general, who seemed as unresponsive as Zach. They took their human burdens outside the building and deposited them safely in the middle of the road.

Soldiers were everywhere, some of them pointing their weapons at the animals among them. Lizbeth saw Tainie standing next to Caitlin, two big cats, one white, one dark. She saw the Scottish soldier who'd said he wanted to be like her. Kevin was nowhere to be seen. She heard him, though.

"Brace yourselves."

The electric sensation eased but didn't completely dissipate. She bent over Zach's body just as a violent concussive blast rent the air and shook the ground. The brick building was sturdy enough to withstand whatever explosives Collins had used, but she was willing to bet the interior of the auditorium had been destroyed.

She didn't really understand what had happened. If she were to guess, she'd say Kevin had figured out how to use the power of the gossamer sphere to erect a force field around Collins, blocking the signal from the trigger device. As soon as the force field dropped, the explosives detonated.

Collins hadn't been lying after all.

Chapter Forty-five

London, England

Despite the resurgence of the electric sensation he associated with the Cataclysm, Zach had forced himself to act. He'd had every intention of killing Agent Collins, but before he could carry it out, the silver fire appeared and he'd found himself unable to move a muscle, not even to blink. He stood there rigidly, unable to breathe, every nerve in his body pulsing painfully. He was aware of what was happening around him but couldn't participate. He knew when the leopard appeared and saw it change into a gorilla. He felt helpless when it carried him out of the building. He'd almost passed out from lack of oxygen, but then right before the explosion, his paralysis vanished.

He gasped and desperately sucked in air, looking up at the concerned face of the little gorilla leaning over him. When he got his breath back, he asked, "Lizbeth?"

She nodded and he sat up, resting his elbows on his knees and looking dazedly around at the soldiers. Three of the agents who'd come in with Collins had been grouped together under guard. Two big cats were walking towards them. One had to be Tainie, but the other?

"Is that Caitlin?" he asked.

Lizbeth nodded again and then tugged at his coat. He muttered, "Oh, sure," and took it off. She put it on, zipped it up, and shifted into herself, bare legs poking out of the bottom of the coat. A soldier standing nearby exclaimed to another soldier, "Bloody hell! Did you see that?"

Lizbeth reached a hand out to Zach's shoulder as he stood. "You're bleeding!"

"I'm okay, really. It's just a scratch. What was that?"

"It was Kevin. He said he activated the sphere." She turned to the white jaguar. "Where is he? Is he all right?"

176

Caitlin lifted her chin towards the building. A chimpanzee was standing at the edge of the roof. He waved cheerily and then climbed down the arborvitae. He started to walk upright, but seemed to find it awkward, so he dropped his knuckles to the ground and swung his legs between his long arms. He stopped next to Lizbeth and gave her a toothy grin.

General Hawthorne, who was sitting on the ground nearby, said, "What the hell happened in there?"

Seamus held up his index finger. "Just a moment, sir, and you'll have your answer."

He unbuttoned his sweater and shrugged it off before draping it over Caitlin's back. She shifted, buttoned the sweater and stood.

"Hello, Marcus," she said, addressing the general. "I'm Caitlin O'Connor, the real one. I knew your grandfather. He was one of us. Were you aware of that?"

General Hawthorne got to his feet and ran a hand over his short hair. He glanced around as if reluctant to admit anything in front of his men. "There were stories passed down, but they were farfetched to say the least."

"And yet something told you they were true."

He shrugged. "I didn't give it much credence until the Cataclysm. Then I *felt* it."

Zach suddenly understood why Seamus had carried the general out of the building. "You're a descendant of the fae like me. I couldn't move in there, either."

Kevin tried to say something, but it came out like typical chimpanzee noises, "Oo-oo ee-ee," and made Zach laugh.

Kevin may not have a human face, but his expression was easy to interpret; it was the same glower of irritation he always gave Zach. He looked around, presumably for something to wear so he could shift back to himself and speak properly. That was when Zach noticed a crowd of people standing in a field beyond the fence. Several of them had cameras pointed in their direction.

Caitlin gestured towards them and said, "Marcus, our friends are among those reporters. Would you be so kind as to allow them to join us? They have our clothing."

In a short amount of time, Bill Masters and a pretty blonde girl had been escorted in.

While Kevin was dressing, it took all Zach's self-control not to laugh at seeing a chimpanzee in boxer shorts. Once Kevin stood before them as himself, he studied the ground, shifting his weight from foot to foot awkwardly. Unlike Seamus, Kevin was clearly uncomfortable as the center of attention. Zach wished he'd get over it and just tell them what happened. He couldn't be the only one itching to find out how Kevin had harnessed the energy of the gossamer sphere.

Instead of an explanation, however, Kevin tilted his head back and raised his eyes to the sky. Zach followed his gaze and shivered at what he saw. He reached out and pulled Lizbeth to his side as three bright fireballs broke through the perpetual post-Cataclysm haze.

Zach had grown up reading all the science fiction classics. He'd seen all the movies and played the video games; immersed himself in fantasy worlds. The best imaginations on the planet had conjured up what it might be like if humanity were a space-faring race. Was that all about to become a reality? Or had they survived the Cataclysm only to face another peril? It was impossible for Zach to think of the future as anything but a new era.

He was just as scared as everyone else, but he'd never been so excited.

The end.